PRAISE FOR

"Hjortsberg gives us a deft, deadly no-let-up narrative in edged p.... as a stropped razor. This one cuts deep so brace yourself." **—WILLIAM F. NOLAN, COAUTHOR OF *LOGAN'S RUN***

"While *fun* might not be the word normally used to describe a story with blood, smoking guns, knives, drugs, death, and heartbreak, you're going to have to trust me on this one. A trip. William Hjortsberg does it again." **—MICHAEL KEATON, GOLDEN GLOBE AWARD-WINNING ACTOR**

"A kick-ass thriller that moves through Mexico like a scalded sidewinder. As always, Hjortsberg delivers wild surprises, cool chatter and raw unforgettable scenes." **—CARL HIAASEN**

"Raymond Chandler, James M. Cain, Jack Kerouac, maybe a little Pynchon— that's the lineage leading to William Hjortsberg and *Mañana*, his nifty tale of murder and young love amid the dark and wilted days of flower power." **—DAVID QUAMMEN, AUTHOR OF *SPILLOVER***

"In the tradition of Hemingway, Hammett and Chandler, Hjortsberg elevates the noir genre through his brilliant use of atmosphere, local color and crackling dialogue, giving us not only a roman noir page-turner but a polaroid-like portrait of the turbulent sixties—drugs, guns and sexually overloaded characters." **—BOB SWAIM, AWARD-WINNING DIRECTOR OF *LA BALANCE, HALF MOON STREET, AND MASQUERADE***

"Alternately hilarious and plain scary . . . [Hjortsberg's] prose is finely wrought, his drama perfect." **—PETER BOWEN, AUTHOR OF *BITTER CREEK***

"A novel of love and desperation . . . Told with a brilliant eye for telling detail, *Mañana* hustles a reader into an exotic world that turns belief upside down." **—RICHARD S. WHEELER, SPUR AWARD-WINNING AUTHOR OF *THE FIRE ARROW***

MAÑANA

BOOKS BY WILLIAM HJORTSBERG

Alp

Gray Matters

Symbiography

Toro! Toro! Toro!

Falling Angel

Tales & Fables

Nevermore

Legend of Darkness (A Screenplay)

Odd Corners: The Slipstream World of William Hjortsberg

Jubilee Hitchhiker: The Life and Times of Richard Brautigan

The Work of Art

Mañana

MAÑANA

A NOVEL

WILLIAM HJORTSBERG

OPEN ROAD

INTEGRATED MEDIA

NEW YORK

Cover design by Mauricio Díaz

978-1-4976-8073-9

Published in 2015 by Open Road Integrated Media, Inc.
345 Hudson Street
New York, NY 10014
www.openroadmedia.com

For Rob and Fred
los amigos que aún no se encuentran

MAÑANA

Tomorrow, and tomorrow, and tomorrow.
—MACBETH

Mañana is soon enough for me.
—PEGGY LEE

MAUNDY
THURSDAY

─ • ● • ─

Deep in the winter after the Summer of Love, the bright bloom of Flower Power faded to black. By the start of *Semana Santa*, the cities north of the border were all on fire. The week before, an unknown assassin gunned down Martin Luther King Jr. in Memphis, and the beautiful nonviolent dream ignited into incendiary nightmare. It all seemed so far away, stoned on the beach at Barra de Navidad in the cowboy state of Jalisco.

My own nightmare began late in the morning of Holy

Thursday when I woke up soaked in blood. My head throbbed with the funereal drumbeat of last night's drugs and booze. I didn't know where the hell I was, disgusted because I thought I'd pissed myself in my sleep. When I went to rub my swollen crusted eyes, I saw my hand, gory as a butcher's. I imagined internal hemorrhage, terrified I'd puked up blood in the night. Handfuls of Percodans washed down with tequila. A night lost to memory.

I recalled Nick easing the spike into my forearm, my first shot of heroin, a skin-pop because I was too chickenshit to mainline. Maybe all that junk ate a hole in my guts. I studied the pebbled concrete ceiling wondering how long it took to bleed to death internally. Then I rolled over and looked straight into Frankie's wide-open eyes. A fat black fly stilt-walked across her turquoise iris. Her throat was cut from ear to ear. More flies gathered like tiny demons feeding along the ragged incision.

Numb from drug excess, I stared at her more out of curiosity than shock. Frankie's corpse might have been some exotic sea creature I'd come across washed up on the beach. She was naked. I studied the spread-winged eagle tattooed across her flaccid breasts trying to remember what had happened. Almost everything following the skin-pop came up a total blank.

After a hundred years, maybe only a few seconds, I struggled to sit, my hangover thundering inside my skull like ninepins falling in hell's bloody bowling alley. The wooden window shutters were closed. The room remained mercifully free from sunlight. A dim dank cave reeking of spilled beer and tequila. Over in the corner, a cheap, unshaded ceramic table lamp with a low-wattage bulb provided dubious illumination. I looked around, more surprised at finding the place deserted than by waking up next to a dead woman. No one had crashed on the two other beds. What was really strange, the room had been stripped clean. The cheap thrift-shop suitcases and piles of dirty clothes, all gone. Along with Nick's bongos, Doc's chess set, the shortwave radio, and a cardboard box full of the Western novels Shank was hooked on.

Hauling myself out of bed felt worse than swimming to the surface in a cesspool full of puss. The effort made my stomach lurch. I staggered into the john and splashed water on my face at the sink, hoping to clear my head. It was like I'd been poisoned. I avoided the grimy mirror and tried putting the pieces back into place. Nothing fit.

I was bare-ass except for the bloody T-shirt but couldn't remember getting undressed. Wandering around in a daze, I located my huaraches and shorts under the bed. The empty sheath for my Randall knife hung from a worn hand-tooled belt lying several feet away. Poking among the gory wadded sheets, I touched Frankie's cold, stiffening legs. Her chilled flesh brought on renewed waves of nausea. I forced myself to do it and found the knife wedged under her buttocks, lacquered with blood.

I had to clean myself up. No way I could face Linda looking like something run through a meat grinder. I went to the front window and opened the shutters a crack. The cherry-red Firebird was gone. Only a vacant parking space outside. Bitter Lemon, my battered VW microbus, always such a sorry short compared to the gangster-mobile, slumped against the curb by the front door to our place on the other side of the wall. The van deserved its nickname. The transmission went out a week after we drove it off the lot. I stared at the California license plate and rotting tail pipe wired up with a coat hanger, all so comfortably familiar. I wanted to replace the unexpected madness with something ordinary. The horror behind me remained palpable in its silence.

I closed the shutters. The sun-bright day outside burned blue-green on my retinas. Made the dim room even darker. I didn't meet Frankie's vacant stare, staggering past her shadow-shrouded corpse to the shower. There was no hot water. In the tropics, even cold felt pleasantly tepid. I stood under the shower's spray and stripped off my T-shirt, wringing out the blood. A thin sliver of deodorant soap was the best I could find. All the shampoo and shaving cream, Dopp kits, razors, and cologne had been cleaned out of the bathroom. I soaped my hair and washed the knife. Last night remained a blank.

I remembered the day back in September when Linda and I realized our time in San Francisco was over. Speed freaks talked in tongues on every street corner. Runaway teenagers hustled spare change outside the supermarket. The whole trip began feeling like an enormous bummer. We decided to split for Mexico and hung with friends in LA for a week or so before rattling across the border just as Hurricane Beulah crashed into Corpus Christi.

Our own weather remained fair and sunny all the way south to San Blas, a place we'd been tipped off about by Santa Cruz surfer buddies. The little coastal town was plagued by swarming gnats and mosquitoes. After two tormented days, we called it quits, driving on toward Guadalajara from where we turned west back down to the coast. A biker in San Blas said to check out Barra de Navidad. We pulled into the isolated seaside village the day Che Guevera got offed in Bolivia.

Barra felt perfect. Small, out of the way, no tourists aside from urban Mexicans down for the weekend; the only gringos, mellow hippies and surfers like us. We found half of a cement-block duplex one street from the beach renting for two hundred pesos a month. It had running water, electricity, and a flush toilet. Twenty-five bucks was a monthly nut within our vagabond budget.

The lukewarm water streaming through my hair and over my face and chest felt magical, only a few degrees cooler than the tropic air. The sultry spray made me imagine I was floating in a Mexican rain cloud. Frankie's blood had been washed away, and the abhorrence lying in the other room seemed as remote as a crater on a distant planet.

Barra had been our haven, the perfect place to write my novel. I worked every morning, and in the afternoons we got high and body-surfed in Melaque Bay, curling waves foaming onto a mile-long crescent of beach. It seemed ideal for the first couple weeks. Right after the *Día de Los Muertos* everything changed, even if we didn't know it at the time. All Saints' Day is a big deal in Mexico. It's a bank holiday and kicks off a three-day festival when people honor their dead, bringing flowers to the graveyard, and building private altars where candles, food, candy, tequila, and a sweet bread called *pan de muerto* are placed alongside photographs of their deceased loved ones.

Linda and I stayed out late that night, eating skull-shaped sugar candy and dancing on the plaza with villagers costumed as cadavers. Back at the pad, we got it on and fell into a dreamless tequila-induced sleep only to be awakened in the dead of night by the sound of someone retching on the other side of the wall behind our bed.

"Sounds like we've got junkies next door," I said to my wife, assuming a hipster's make-believe savvy. Turned out I was right on the money. Our unseen neighbors puked all day long and through our following sleepless night. Linda and I muttered about how hard it must be to kick. We might as well have been discussing molecular biology.

On the second morning when I opened the shutters to greet the always surprising early morning bustle, I encountered Nick, shirtless, leaning out his window next door smoking a cigarette. He looked to be in his late thirties, about ten years older than me. With his mustache and black hair combed straight back off his forehead, Nick could have been a youthful Cesar Romero. A vivid tattoo of a spider weaving its web across his right deltoid was enhanced by the pallor underlying his tawny complexion. He had a broad engaging smile and an easygoing manner. We started talking and hit it off right away. Just another chance encounter, fellow travelers in the third world. Before the day was over, this total stranger was my new best friend.

Linda and I started hanging out next door. Nick was a Gemini, Frankie a Libra. A good pair. His dual nature balanced by her impartiality. Nick had a Zenith Transoceanic that drew in the jazz stations from L.A. and San Diego, and he'd beat a Latin counterpoint rhythm on his bongos to the improvisations of Miles, Monk, and Zoot Sims. Told me he'd played with Art Pepper in San Quentin. I assumed he'd been sent up for junk like a lot of musicians. It never occurred to me to think of him as a criminal.

Linda and Frankie bonded right from the start. A Mount Holyoke girl and a hooker, opposites attracting like magnets. You could tell Frankie had once been a beautiful woman. Booze and drugs had eroded her youth like sand storms blurring the features of the Sphinx. She told Linda that she only turned tricks to score a fix. She said she hadn't had her period in ten years because of using heroin. My wife couldn't get enough of that kind of shit.

Nick and Frankie might have kicked, but they weren't exactly clean. They got stoned on codeine and various painkillers scored without prescriptions at the corner *farmacia*. From time to time, friends in the States sent spoonfuls of white powder folded in slips of paper inside airmail letters. And, there was always weed. Linda and I brought a couple lids in with us from L.A. Got a big laugh out of that, smuggling dope *into* Mexico. We burned through our little stash in under three weeks. Then, it was catch-as-catch-can, scoring smoke on the beach from other wayfarers like us.

It felt risky even after hooking-up with Memo, a teenager from Guadalajara, who packed a *bolsa*-load of pot on the bus to Barra every weekend. Nick didn't dig Memo at all. Said he was a gutter punk, the kind Federales kept their eye on. Said he was poison, would rat us all out for a peso. Nick found some

Indian kid down from the mountains and made a deal to buy twenty-five kilos.

"It's Michoacán," he said. "The best. No more copping on the beach."

The price was five hundred pesos. Splitting it meant twenty bucks for me and Linda. Weed went for a hundred dollars a key in Frisco. Seemed like a good investment. Nick didn't have a car so I went to pick up the load of mota, driving south toward Colima and turning off before the city onto the Paso de Potrerillos road. The potholed pavement ended at the Michoacán border. From there, it was more like driving on a dry streambed. My directions were to look for the kid waiting by the side of the road after three or four miles.

Solemn under his straw sombrero, he stood in the shade of a mango tree with two skinny horses. I locked the van and rode for about an hour up a narrow trail into the unknown, chafing on the wooden saddle. We dismounted by a palm frond-roofed *palapa* where the Indian kid's mother squatted, brewing coffee on a charcoal fire, her new baby, wrapped in a rebozo, slung hammock-fashion across her back.

They fed me tamales and coffee with sweetened condensed milk like the guest of honor. This made me nervous. After waiting most of the afternoon, I regretted being alone in the jungle with all that money. Two men arrived late in the day, wearing machetes at their waists and leading a burro packed with a large burlap-wrapped bale. I felt electric with adrenaline. After a handshake, I gave them the cash, all *buenos amigos* now. The kid and I rode back to my van with the big bundle. It was past nine at night by the time I returned to Barra.

MAÑANA

We made a party out of cleaning the shit, setting the unwrapped bale on a sheet of cardboard. Nick found several boards somewhere, laying them on top. We drank beer and danced on the boards to the throb of the Transoceanic. By dawn, we had it all reduced to bowls of herb, a shoe box full of seeds and twin tumbleweed clusters of twigs and stems, which I drove out of town and tossed under the palm trees where the paved road began.

Our share filled an empty five-kilo Nido powdered milk tin. Made me feel like Pretty Boy Floyd or Jesse James. A cool desperado riding through the night. That romantic outlaw trail led straight to Frankie, bled-out on the bed in the other room.

I wanted to stay in the shower forever, lost in the spray of a tropical waterfall. Stomach-turning spasms of fear brought me back to the silent terror behind the door. I turned off the faucet. There were no towels. I padded naked into the other room leaving a track of wet footprints across the smooth concrete floor. Wrapping the Randall in my clean-rinsed T-shirt, I slipped into my shorts and car tire–soled huaraches. In the kitchen, I peeked through an opening in the back shutters. Other than a couple pacing chickens, all was quiet. No sign of the landlord's family on the low adobe veranda across the sandy backyard.

I grabbed my belt and sheath before sneaking out the back door and up the steps onto the roofed-over porch behind our place. Safe on a folding chair by the oilcloth-covered card table, I felt like I'd just crossed the border from a foreign country. The porch had a simple concrete sink just like the dreary walled-in kitchen next door. The two little apartments shared identical floor plans except ours wasn't completely enclosed. More pleasant cooking and eating in the open air. My familiar world, always so safe and comfortable, now felt pregnant with silent menace, contaminated by evil. The future stretched ahead like an empty wasteland. What would I say to Linda? There's a dead woman next door. I can't remember if I killed her. Sorry I stayed out all night.

I held my breath and went inside. The room contained the same shadowy gloom as the death chamber beyond the wall. "Linda," I whispered, getting no answer. It was close to noon. I didn't hit the light switch. In the always-shuttered junky pad, lightbulbs burned day and night. I opened our shutters and let sunlight in. The bed had not been used. Maybe she went to the beach. Sat drinking a beer someplace. I peeked into an empty bathroom. "Linda . . . ?"

Sitting on the bed feeling oddly relieved, it hit me what was wrong. Linda's clothes were gone. Shoes, jewelry, makeup, all the bathroom stuff, the woven *bolsas* she used as luggage and her leather shoulder bag. Not one trace of Linda remained. What did this mean? Our VW waited outside. My wife either left on the local bus or in the gangster-mobile. Shank and Doc held the keys to the Firebird. Nick was doubtless along for the ride.

Everything came up blank. Why was I left behind? Maybe I killed Frankie and they tossed me to the dogs. Or the real murderer made me the fall guy. You had to get caught to be the fall guy. I had time on my side. No one knew Frankie was dead. A dark unknown dread suffused the ordinary with terror. Everything came into sharper focus. I'd never felt so vital and alive.

MAÑANA

❁

I packed everything in under fifteen minutes, stripping the porch kitchen first while the landlord's yard remained still and empty. The table, chairs, and Coleman stove were folded and stashed inside. Next, all the cooking stuff, plates, and utensils went into the orange crates we used for storage. I piled them on the bed and returned to the back steps, lifting my soon-to-be-abandoned corrugated garbage pail aside to dig the Nido tin full of pot out of the sand with a soupspoon.

I closed and locked the back door. Clothes got stuffed into a war-surplus duffel. The portable typewriter nested in a clever self-containing case. My toolkit and a carton of paperbacks sat by the street entrance. I bundled my so-called novel, stripped the sheets and pillows from the bed, and rolled up the Two Gray Hills rug Linda bought at the Old Faithful Hamilton store on our way to Frisco in the summer of '65.

Out onto the dirt street, hit by the full fire of the midday sun, I felt anxious to be on my way. None of the sparse foot traffic took any notice of a gringo packing his gear. Everything fit into a big storage compartment out of sight under the van's foam-covered sleeping platform. I'd built a set of shelves against the far wall. It had rails like on a ship, to keep stuff from sliding off. After one last look around inside, I locked the door behind me and drove off with the key.

On the way out of town, I pulled over at the ice factory on the corner of the plaza. All the carnival rides waited like resting skeletons before their nighttime dance. I bought five kilos of ice for the cooler. My filtered water was almost gone. The near-empty bottle and two pesos got me a new twenty-five-liter supply.

When Doc and Shank first showed up in the red Pontiac, the plaza looked more like an empty parking lot. They rolled in sometime mid-January, high on downers, and the slow-motion party began. The gangsters bumped around like zombies for days. Nick turned into another person, someone underwater. The junk came from a pharmacy they'd broken into on the way down.

Shank, a wiry little man, had a way of showing both his uppers and lowers like a skull when he smiled. A double-Scorpio with a moon in Cancer, not the happiest of horoscopes. His real name was Burt Breitenbach. I never knew the others' last names. Doc was a pudgy old guy in his fifties. He'd been married to a mob boss's daughter, managed a casino in Vegas, and had thirty tailor-made suits in his closet. When his father-in-law learned he was a junky, Doc got kicked out on his ass to fend for himself. Doc wasn't much good at that.

All of them, genial Nick included, were parole violators. They'd each been inside for a ten-year stretch though not in the same joint. They went in listening to Frank Sinatra and came out to find the Beatles topping the charts in a strange new world. Linda called them "secondhand gangsters."

Doc and Shank hooked up in L.A. and robbed a Beverly Hills jewelry store with another guy who was supposed to drive the getaway car. When the alarm went off early, the driver panicked and peeled out of the parking garage across the street, leaving his partners holding a satchel full of Patek Philippes and the wallet of a customer surprised while paying for his purchase. With no time to grab anything else, Shank and Doc ran for the parking garage. They tossed their Saturday-night specials down a storm drain as the fuzz roared up outside the jewelers. Finding no car, they slipped out the back and into a Hertz office down the block where they rented a convertible with a credit card from the stolen wallet.

Dumb luck stayed with them even after they ditched the rental outside San Bernardino and hot-wired an unlocked Firebird. That same evening, the fugitive pair broke through the skylight of a pharmacy in Wickenburg, Arizona, scoring a little cash from the register and a bunch of drugs and hypodermic needles. Before leaving the premises, Shank and Doc had to fix. They shot up a bottle of Demerol and passed out, awakened in the morning by the sound of the front door unlocking. The slimmest of miracles allowed them to scramble out onto the roof before the mess was discovered. "The bungling burglars," Linda joked behind their backs.

Driving out of Barra for the last time added false nostalgia to the putrid stew of my mood. Shank always dressed in black. Black turtleneck, black watch cap, black trousers. He naturally complained of the heat and asked Linda to turn his pants into cut-offs. When she finished the alterations, Shank made an appearance dressed exactly the same including the knitted hat. His skinny white legs stuck out of the knee-length shorts like the shinbones of a skeleton.

"How do I look?" he rasped.

Picturing Shank at that moment, I found it hard to believe Linda had willingly run off with such losers. Maybe she was just with Nick? What if she saw me kill Frankie and wanted to get away? If one of the others did it, maybe he took her along because she'd seen too much. The passed-out fall guy had missed the whole thing.

I drove ten miles to Cihuatlán, pulling up before the bank, a squat stone building on the main drag. It was just before they closed for siesta. I got my papers together, locked the van, and went inside to draw out my money.

"*Perdón, señor,*" the pretty young teller said. I didn't catch it all but made out "*su esposa,*" and "*esta mañana temprano,*" and realized she was talking about a withdrawal earlier in the day.

"*¿Cuánto?*" I asked.

"*Todo.*"

I left the bank like a robot. Linda had cleaned out our account. More than five hundred dollars. All that remained from the twelve hundred bucks we'd worked our asses off for, typing on Flexowriters in the financial district nine-to-five to fund a long stay in paradise. Back behind the wheel, I made a tally of my assets. I had nearly a tank of gas. About eighty pesos in paper and coin in my pocket after buying the ice and water. Two emergency twenties were rubber-banded behind the sun visor in case of traffic stops. Handy for the little everyday bribes Mexicans called the *mordida.* That came to maybe fifteen bills American. My slim personal fortune also included five kees of clean killer weed. I'd have to get to Guad before seeing any cash out of that.

Thinking about dope in my car made me glance up the street toward the cop shop. Captain Guzmán slouched against the peeling wall outside in his wrinkled khaki uniform. He chewed on a toothpick, cap visor pulled low on his forehead, staring straight ahead. I knew he'd seen me, just as I knew he kept the hammer of his holstered .45 automatic on half-cock. I'd become acquainted with the captain when Doc had a beef over a bar tab, claiming he'd been charged twice for his drinks. The *patrón* said Doc pulled a knife, an offense landing the old man in the Cihuatlán jail.

Somehow I became the go-between and drove over every day from Barra hoping to straighten things out. Doc had it pretty good. He tipped a kid a peso each time for bringing his meals from a local cantina. I supplied enough downers to keep him mellow. Doc needed to pay up but refused to unbutton his change purse. One day, I came over and found his cell empty.

Captain Guzmán was the man in charge. I'd seen enough of him to be afraid. When I asked about Doc, he grinned around his toothpick and said the *viejo* had been moved to Autlán de Navarro, the municipal capital.

"*Más duro en Autlán,*" Guzmán said.

Much tougher in Autlán. The captain's words stayed with me as I drove up the twisting hairpin mountain road toward the birthplace of Carlos Santana. The Palacio Municipal stood on one side of the Jardín Hidalgo. I parked a block away. Barred iron grates set in the stone sidewalk let down light into a subterranean dungeon beneath the temple of justice. I called out to Doc, and he hurried from the gloom, pale, harried, his drip-dry beige suit soiled and tattered.

He was desperate to get out. Because he was too old to fuck, a couple *machitos* had tied a string to his dick and yanked him around like a burro all night long. I said it might take every penny, and he shoved two hundred bucks in traveler's checks up through the grate, claiming it was his entire stake. I found a lawyer who got him off for 150 dollars. Doc kissed and fondled the five traveler's checks I gave back to him like they were a relic of Christ. It wasn't that he lacked resources. He and Shank still had a satchel full of thousand-dollar watches.

Remembering Doc's ordeal made me want to get as far away from Captain Guzmán as possible, pronto. I popped Bitter Lemon into gear, cruising out of town without looking back. I didn't feel safe until I was nearly to Manzanillo and pulled off the road to roll a big, fat dorf. Funny how I coined that name. We had this huge pile of Michoacán and no rolling papers. Cigarettes were so cheap in Mexico no one rolled his own. You never saw a pipe smoker. We unraveled the tobacco from store-bought smokes and stuffed the empty paper tubes with mota. After experimenting with different sorts of paper cut to size, I found the outer wrappers of our Waldorf toilet tissue twisted up just fine, burning smooth and easy. When I rolled the first one for the gang next door, the letters DORF ran along the length of the joint like a trademark.

Killer shit. Three or four hits got me stoned out of my gourd. Mission accomplished. Back on the highway, I felt better with every mile I put between me and stiff, cold Frankie, far off in Barra. I didn't want to think about the mess I was in. Not yet. Why bring myself down? Better to clunk along in my dream world, random thoughts drifting through the corners of my mind like wind-blown gossamer. After Shank and Doc showed up, everything changed. Calmed by weed, our scene became something of a hipster sitcom: amiable ex-cons living next door to the innocent young couple so curious to taste every drop of real life.

Most of the time, Linda and I were the squares made hip to the ways of the underworld by our criminal neighbors. Just once, we sat in the driver's seat. Friends in Frisco sent us thirty hits of windowpane folded inside a copy of *Zap Comix No. 1*, a wacky offbeat comic book. The gangsters had never done LSD. One more social change missed during a decade in stir, along with the pill, the civil rights movement, and men in space.

The blotter acid was laid out in five rows of six doses. I cut off the top row with scissors and clipped it into individual hits. The gangsters acted pretty cool about taking their first trip, thinking it would be like any other drug. They knew all about narcotics. Acid was different. I warned them not to pig out on food before they dropped. Linda and I fasted all day, going next door at dusk.

We lit candles around the room. Nick found some mellow sounds on his shortwave. I passed out the hits, instructing the gang to chew them well and swallow the pulp. Waiting for the mysterious is always momentous. I enjoyed watching our new friends cope with the unspoken stress. Frankie stretched out on the bed staring silently at the ceiling. Nick sat in the corner tapping softly on his bongos. Linda brewed herbal tea in the kitchen with Doc hovering around her, pretending to help. Only Shank betrayed any apprehension, pacing back and forth like a caged panther.

A couple hours later, their cool impenetrable facades crumbled like sugar cubes in water when the fluid psychedelic onrush swept over them. Impossible to deny five hundred mics of pure lysergic acid surging through your system. All barriers dissolved. Sound became tangible. Solid surfaces appeared porous. You were on your own, a solitary traveler into the unknown.

Fear and acid don't mix. Paranoia taps into the dark primal terror within. Drop ten milligrams of Valium before you trip or risk a descent into deep despair. Lost in my own inner wonderland, I lurched around the two-room apartment, observing the bold outlaws stripped bare to the core. Linda lay on the bed hugging Frankie who wept like the little girl she'd left behind years ago. Nick found a new station on his Transoceanic and pounded the bongos to a violent Afro-Cuban beat until his fingertips bled.

In the moldy enclosed kitchen, Doc sat at the table slicing vegetables with a cheap serrated knife. He wanted to make a stew. Doc was a great admirer of Kahlil Gibran and quoted snatches from *The Prophet* as he chopped carrots into ever-smaller pieces. "'Yesterday is but today's memory and tomorrow is today's dream,'" he mumbled, wielding his knife. "'Trust . . .'" Mumble, mumble. "'Dreams . . .'" Chop, chop. "'Eternity . . .'"

Back in the other room, I sat on the edge of the bed. My wife comforted a weeping prostitute while I listened to the insane throb of Nick's drumming. I glanced over into the corner where Shank crouched, wild-eyed, grinning like the label on a poison bottle. "What you lookin' at, you little fuck," he demanded.

"Nothing," I said.

"So, now I'm nothing," Shank spat at me. "That what you think, pretty boy?"

I tried to disarm the situation before things got out of hand. Shank cut me off. "You look at a man in the joint like that," he snarled, "and you're asking for a shiv stuck between your ribs."

I said I was sorry. Shank narrowed his eyes. His voice dropped a notch lower into menace. "There was this one son-of-a-bitch in Folsom always giving me the look," he said, every word etched with dread. "He bunked on the bottom tier. They unlocked the cellblock one row at a time when we went for chow or out in the yard. I set it up with a buddy to steal a can of gas from the motor shop. He was just ahead of me in line and tossed that shit into the prick's cell as he walked past. I had a book of matches. Tell you what, matches 're worth more 'n cigarettes in the can. I lit up the whole book and said, 'Who you lookin' at now, fuckface?' Tossed in the matches and walked on to the mess hall. Flames blasted out through the bars like a tornado from hell. Fried that bastard crisp as a slice of bacon."

Shank said all this slow and steady, enunciating each word as if carving it on my tombstone. His lidded eyes never blinked. "Guess that took care of him," I muttered as the floor swirled like rainbows under my feet.

"You let a man disrespect you and get away with it," Shank said, his burning, slitted eyes fixed on me, "you ain't nothin' but a piece a shit for all the world to fuck."

I smiled awkwardly at Burt Breitenbach and went back into the kitchen to listen to Doc quoting pop-culture aphorisms. The menace lurked in the other room like some demon waiting to swallow me whole. Doc had diced a bunch of carrots into molecular bits on the tabletop and was crashing around in a rage. He poked at a week's worth of filthy clay pots and plastic dishes heaped in the concrete sink.

"How can you stand to live like this?" he roared. "It's different for us. We're on the lam. I'd rather be back in stir. I kept my cell clean. Not like this filthy hippie shit!"

I told Doc that Linda kept our pad next door neat as his beloved fucking cell. All this negativity was bringing me down. I slipped out the back and went for a long walk on the beach. A full moon rode high in the velvet tropic sky, casting a wavering silver path across the restless sea. It hit me like the Sistine Chapel painted by Bach. I wanted to take the pyrotechnics of my trip far away from all the gangster craziness.

By the time I got back, I was starting to come down, acid visions surging in ever-diminishing waves. All was dark and quiet next door. I spotted the aurora borealis flare of a candle through our open window and stepped inside to find Linda sitting naked on the bed. "Hi, Tod," she said, candlelight glinting in her green eyes and making her reddish hair glow like burnished copper. "Missed you."

Memories of our acid-fueled candle-lit lovemaking had me confused. Either Linda had run out on me, taking up with Nick and the others, or else she was their hostage, a replacement for Frankie, and they'd stolen all our money. If the first was true, I should make a run for the border on the double. But the slimmest possibility of her being a prisoner of someone like Shank made that impossible. There was no other choice. I had to find her. Somehow, some way, I had to get my wife back.

A bit after three in the afternoon, I rattled into Colima, a pretty palm-shaded colonial town with twin snowcapped volcanoes towering ten miles distant. Along with Chihuahua and Oaxaca, Colima was the capital of a state with the same name. So good they named it twice, like New York, New York, my hometown. I'd only been here once before, about a month ago when Bitter Lemon needed more transmission work. The only certified VW dealership in the area was located in Colima. When the gang heard I was going, they put in a big order for downers. They'd worn out their welcome at local *farmacias* as far afield as Manzanillo. A sorry achievement in the casual, no-prescriptions-needed atmosphere of Mexican drugstores.

They wanted Percodan or Hycodan. While the microbus sat in the repair shop, I wandered with a shopping bag from pharmacy to pharmacy, buying all the available narcotics. I got a surreal kick out of sweeping six or eight bottles of synthetic opiates off the countertops into my sack. No one refused when I asked for the drugs. Nick had given me several hundred pesos. Barely half of it was spent before I tapped Colima dry. I drove back to Barra with more than forty bottles of painkillers, the big sugar man with a load of candy for his friends next door.

I figured my "friends" had gone on to Guadalajara after cleaning out my bank account. They knew a contact there who'd buy the stolen watches. Only two roads up to the big city, one through Colima or the shorter route by way of Autlán. I parked on a side street behind the cathedral and backtracked to all the *farmacias* I could remember, pretending to be looking for my cousin and his wife. My description of Nick and Linda got no results. I struck out everywhere. I threw Doc and Shank into the mix as an uncle and his friend, without luck. They'd obviously gone the other way. If they'd come through Colima, I knew they would have tried to score.

I walked back to the Jardín Libertad. A guy with a pushcart sold *tuba* out in front of the cathedral. Naturally fermented sap from a coconut palm, *tuba* had a sweet alcoholic tingle. "*Sin hielo,*" I said, not trusting the ice was pure. He ladled out a tall glassful.

"*¿Cacahuates?*" the vendor asked, wanting to sprinkle chopped peanuts on top. I shook my head and paid him a peso, crossing the street to sit on a cast iron bench where he could see I wasn't going to run off with his glass. A pair of mangy emaciated pariah dogs, so common in rural Mexico, sniffed along the gutter. The plantain vendor's steam whistle screamed like a demon from hell behind me in the plaza. I hadn't eaten all day. The first mouthful of *tuba* caught in my gorge and I nearly puked.

I had to cram some food into my lurching gut and found a tiled sandwich joint on a side street. After wolfing down a *torta al pastor* with avocado, I had them wrap another to go. It set me back three pesos. I needed to watch expenses until I scratched up more bread. Coming across a corner stationery store, I bought their cheapest postal scale for eighteen pesos. At a supermarket in the commercial district, I spent more precious *dinero* on a box of plastic sandwich bags and four bottles of Pacífico, my favorite Mexican beer.

On the outskirts of town, I stopped at a Pemex station and topped off my tank with twelve liters of ninety-octane Gasolmex from the green pump. This cost another eight pesos and change. I was down to about ten bucks liquid capital.

Back behind the wheel, I headed along Highway 110 toward the two tapering volcanoes. Colima became a distant mirage in my rearview mirror. I fired up a dorf, popped the cap on a *cerveza*, and found a radio station playing *ranchera* music.

The road wound up into the mountains. Bitter Lemon chugged along, not setting any speed records. Didn't matter much to me. No point getting anyplace in a hurry. Had no idea where I'd find Linda. Didn't have any sort of plan. All I could do was get to wherever I was going. Every time I started coming down, I pulled over and twisted up another joint. I laid off the beer, saving it as a treat for when I stopped for the night.

Past midnight, the road approached Tuxcueca, a village on the southern shore of Lake Chapala. I turned left, avoiding the scattering of lights. After a couple more miles, I came to a narrow dirt lane leading down toward the lake. Worth a chance and I took it, driving to a secluded spot. The night air felt cold wearing shorts. I pulled on a sweater and sat on a rock by the water's edge to eat my second sandwich. A nearly full moon shone over the still black surface of the lake. Flecks of pale light winked at my dilemma.

After finishing the soggy *torta*, I rummaged under the van's sleeping platform for my tequila bottle. A couple snorts and a big fat dorf might ease my thoughts. Pulling the Zippo from my pocket, I came up with the key to our place in Barra. I hurled it out into the lake. It fell ten yards from shore, a soft *plop* in the moon's rippling reflected light. I lit up and took a deep toke.

A slug from the bottle burned its way down, leaving me none the wiser. Funny, remembering the past in such detail. All the whacko gangster misadventures, every odd detail for six months, each ticking second of today from the first moment I woke up lying next to Frankie's corpse. What I couldn't recall was everything after Nick shot the smack under my skin last night. It was like trying to bring back a dream.

GOOD
FRIDAY

— • ● • —

I was awake at first light, haunted by nightmares. Visions of Linda sprawled in a filthy bed with her throat cut stayed with me as I staggered out into the daylight. Once she took our money from the bank, the gangsters had no further use for my wife. She'd be a liability. Why would a classy chick like Linda travel with a bunch of second-rate deadbeats? She'd stand out like a nun in a whorehouse. Draw too much attention. Shank wouldn't like that. What if Linda gave him the wrong look? Would he set her on fire?

Splashing cold lake water on my face cleared away the bad dreams. I pumped up the Coleman stove and started a pot of coffee. While it perked, I unfolded the card table and a wooden chair. More water heated for shaving in a saucepan on the other burner. The first cup of hot black java felt like a Benzedrine hit.

I unsheathed the death knife, a Randall Model 11 Alaskan Skinner, and diced a last hunk of cheese from the cooler. My father ordered the knife in 1952, when the blade first appeared in Bo Randall's catalog out of Orlando, Florida. The price tag was twenty dollars. Dad had some fantasy about going big-game hunting in Alaska or Montana or someplace. He imagined skinning trophy elk and bear with his hand-forged knife. I was twelve and dreamed of going with him into the wilderness. Six months later, in November, he died without warning from a massive heart attack before the coveted Randall arrived. Mom gift-wrapped the knife and put it under the Christmas tree for me with his name on the card.

The Skinner had a broad five-inch carbon steel blade sharp enough for surgery, holding an edge even after cutting into bone. Chopping cheddar was a breeze. A shudder of revulsion ran through me. How easily did the Randall slice Frankie's throat? Distracted, I slipped and slashed open my thumb. I ignored the immediate pain, staring at my blood as it dripped all over the cheese. A fitting meal for a murderer.

After stanching my wound with a Band-Aid from the medicine kit, I considered tossing the gory cheddar but couldn't afford to waste food and rinsed it clean in the lake. Linda had stored some leftover rice and beans in a Tupperware container. I heated them in the skillet topped with the cheddar and fried a couple eggs. A hot breakfast didn't change anything. I still felt trapped in the lowest reaches of hell.

Unable to shake a pervading sense of doom, I shaved my two-day stubble and washed the kitchen stuff lakeside with Dr. Bronner's liquid soap. After pulling the Nido can from its hiding place, I mechanically filled plastic sandwich bags with mota, weighing each bag on the postal scale. Twenty-eight grams equaled an ounce. I didn't try for perfection. Anything around thirty grams did the trick.

The work grew tedious after the first twenty bags. Setting fire to a dorf took the edge off the dull assembly-line routine. Fill and weigh; fill and weigh; twist the flap around, sealing the baggie in a neat bundle. The process became mechanical. I drifted back to the start of *Semana Santa*, looking for missing pieces in the fucking puzzle.

The approach of Holy Week turned Barra de Navidad from a sleepy backwater into a boomtown. A carnival set up its rickety Ferris wheel and whirling nausea-inducing spin rides on the dusty plaza in front of the scaffold-enclosed church. Crowds started rolling in by the Saturday before Palm Sunday. Barra's population increased tenfold. These weren't gringo tourists but lower middle-class Mexicans. Guadalajara cab drivers bringing their wives and girlfriends down for a frolic on the beach.

Crepe-paper decorated taco stands competed with women

frying churros on every street corner. Oyster sellers shucked succulent bivalves out of ice-filled buckets in a movable feast, weaving through the joyous throng. Other ice-bucket entrepreneurs sold beer and soft drinks and cold slices of watermelon. *Rasparadores* hawking shaved ice snow cones in paper cups, pushed wheeled carts, shouting, "*¡Nieves! ¡Nieves!*"

Caught up in the frenzy, Linda and I rode the carnival rides and danced to mariachi bands under the strands of colored lights strung about the plaza. The gangsters went at it like they'd never partied before. With all the booze and drugs, no one crashed until after four in the morning. I had to drop a red to get any sleep. By Holy Tuesday, the insanity reached a fever pitch. The insistent clatter of *matracas*, a satanic castanet concerto, got us all jumpy. Everyone went nuts.

I caught Linda making out with a stranger on the dilapidated merry-go-round. When she saw me watching, she laughed hysterically, shrill and raucous, some wild jungle creature. She said she owed me one. Frankie started a flirtation with a fisherman at a third-rate cantina down by the lagoon. Nick and Shank dragged her out, holding off the drunken crowd at knifepoint.

Later, Shank showed me his weapon, a wicked curve-bladed linoleum cutter, recounting the dramatic showdown. "Wasn't my kind of play at all," he said, exposing all his teeth in something between a sneer and a grimace. "Had to back up my buddy. If we'd done it my way, we'd of got us a couple two-by-fours and waited outside that shit-hole until the son-of-a-bitch come staggering out. Tell you what. Beat a man right and he'll never forget you."

MAÑANA

Wednesday night of Holy Week, we all stayed home. Frankie was grounded. The party roared on around her. Four crazed nights, fueled by narcotics and alcohol, had led us into the land of the walking dead. Staggering zombies, our eyes revealed a shared paranoia. You could see the cogwheels turning. Everyone was so wired you didn't want to catch their glance for more than a fleeting second. In a room full of lunatics, keep your gaze fixed on the floor.

We had all the booze, smoke, and pills any six deadbeats might desire. If we wanted food or sweets, we could open the front window and order from the vendors passing outside. Except we didn't. If tacos or slices of melon were desired, a delegate, usually me, was dispatched out into the throng. A fog of marijuana smoke obscured the room. We feared open shutters might betray our hazy asylum to the festive world outside and kept the private party to ourselves, manic, bottled-up, claustrophobic, a sextet of neurotics pretending to have fun, going through the motions, sleepwalkers on a treadmill.

After an hour, I twisted the final baggie tight, one hundred in all. A nice stash remained at the bottom of the Nido can. I poured the oregano out of a quart-size Tupperware container and refilled it most of the way with mota. Packed the sealed plastic bags in the five-gallon can, layering them like sardines. Tamping down the lid, I returned the can to its hiding place in the van and rolled a day's smoke. I lined the joints up in an old Between the Acts cigar tin I used as a "cigarette" case.

Past midnight early in Holy Thursday, Nick unveiled his surprise. A folded-paper packet of heroin had arrived in an Easter card that morning at the post office via *Lista de Correos*. "Who's up for a little nightcap?" he laughed. The other smackers crowded around in disbelief, wondering why he'd left anything for them.

I watched Nick cook the junk in a teaspoon over a candle flame. When it liquefied and bubbled, he siphoned the spoonful up with an eyedropper and attached a hypodermic needle. "Let's take a ride on a horse," he grinned.

I'd always been a conscientious objector to hard drugs. Four days of straight partying lowered my resistance. "Not in my vein," I said. Nick stuck me with the needle, and I felt a warm rush run like honey ants up inside my arm, exploding into my brain with a skyrocket burst of serene, secure contentment. I lay back on the unmade bed watching in a dreamy haze as the others lined up for their fix. I can't remember if Linda shot up or ever seeing Nick fixing for that matter. I was lost in the lush gardens of Xanadu.

It took under an hour to drive to Guadalajara, past Jocotepec at the western end of the lake, enough time to light up and forget about dead whores. The first sign of civilization came after FIN DEL PAVIMENTO. Federal jurisdiction over the highway ended, and colorful commercial advertising blossomed among the garbage dump slums scarring the outskirts of town. Nailed to every tree, tin TOME COKE and CARTA BLANCA signs were the only bright spots amid acres of corrugated shanties. Whitewashed stone walls bore faded slogans from the last presidential election: PROGRESSO Y PAZ CON DÍAZ-ORDAZ. The political acronyms, PRI and PAN, blighted backyard auto-repair shops and the small neighborhood stores known as *tiendas*. Five stenciled interlinking Olympic circles appeared almost everywhere to celebrate the summer games coming to Mexico City in October.

I had only been in Guad three times before and retraced the route taken on my last couple visits, following the highway into the city to Avenida Adolfo López Mateos Sur. It was called Avenida de los Ingenieros back in 1964 on my first trip with Linda. Turned right onto Avenida Niños Héroes. Took a left at the great glass slab of the Hilton and drove a few blocks along Avenida 16 de Septiembre toward the historic district. The twin spires of the domed cathedral looked to be a single tower as I turned right onto Madero and left on Corona, parking across from the Hotel Fenix.

I'd been here twice this year. In the middle of February, when our 180-day tourist cards had only three weeks left to run, Linda and I confronted the daunting prospect of driving north to the border and crossing back into the States in order to gain an additional six months. The other option was to see a guy Nick knew in Guad. He called him "Freddy of the Fenix." Playing it straight and doing things legal meant an uncomfortable thousand-mile round-trip drive and maybe four hundred bucks out of pocket. The crooked path involved a quick Guadalajara trip to buy black-market tourist cards for half that price from this character known only as Freddy.

Easy choice. Right after Valentine's Day, I drove to Guad on my first visit to the Hotel Fenix. Nick said to ask the door-man for Freddy. I did and was told to go into the lobby and wait. It seemed like some pulp magazine fantasy. I sat in a wide brightly lit room tiled in slabs of frozen butterscotch. All that gleaming onyx made me dizzy. I shut my eyes and dozed off.

A gentle tapping brought me instantly alert. An hour had passed. A plump middle-aged Mexican businessman loomed over me, his skin pink and smooth like he'd been sculpted from Spam. Well-trimmed mustache. Slicked-back hair, black as polished obsidian. Freddy had the pampered look of the little man on top of the wedding cake. He wore an impecca-bly tailored gray mohair suit and a maroon silk Sulka tie. His gold-and-lapis cufflinks matched the ring gleaming on his little finger. I felt out of place. A tramp invading the palace.

"I am Freddy," he said in a soft melodic voice. "How may I be of service to you?" He spoke with the polite formality of a diplomat.

I told him about our soon-to-expire tourist cards.

"This is not the place to discuss such matters," Freddy purred. "Why not join me for some refreshment at my home?" He turned on calfskin-shod feet, agile as a dancer.

I followed him out of the hotel. A burly goon in a pink leisure suit with bellbottom trousers stood by a sleek black Mercedes sedan, his shirt open to reveal a thick gold chain glittering among his bristling black chest hair. He held the rear door open for Mr. Freddy, not giving me a second glance as he went around and got in on the driver's side. I didn't know if I was supposed to sit up front next to him. Fuck it, I thought, stepping out on the street and climbing into the back beside the boss. This big guy was no mere chauffeur. He was Freddy's muscle.

The luxurious car slid through the crowded streets of Guadalajara, sounds of traffic silenced by tinted windows. Freddy wasn't much for small talk. He stared straight ahead, humming "Malagueña Salerosa" under his breath as if I wasn't even there. Playing it cool, I ignored him, concentrating on the back of the bodyguard's thick neck.

Freddy lived on a sloping hillside in Zapopan, a northwestern suburb. We drove along various unfamiliar streets impossible to remember. Freddy's house was a modern single-story glass-and-concrete box. The monotonous terrazzo floors were brightened by handwoven Oaxacan rugs. Bold Huichol yarn paintings hung on the walls. The furniture was all chrome with leather upholstery and slabs of polished black marble. Grimacing Zapotec funeral urns lined a bookshelf like a demonic rogues gallery.

We sat on opposite sides of a thick rectangle of midnight flecked with mica constellations. Smelling sickly sweet as a funeral parlor, three white gardenia blossoms floated in a water-filled crystal bowl at the center of the table. The somber thug lurked somewhere behind me, his menacing presence an unseen reminder of my vulnerability. Freddy asked to see some identification. I passed over my California driver's license, Linda's expired passport, and our nearly defunct tourist cards.

While Freddy jotted notes, an old Indian woman dressed in black brought a silver tray holding two cups of steaming coffee along with a small pitcher of scalded milk and brown sugar cubes in a bowl. I sipped coffee and watched the plump criminal wield his cigar-size fountain pen. *"Bueno,"* he said when done, capping the Mont Blanc with fussy precision. "The cost for you will be two thousand pesos."

I peeled the money out of my wallet and slid it across the table, wondering if I'd ever get what I was paying for. Freddy thumbed through the cash like a bank teller and slipped it into a slim Cartier billfold. Nothing more was said about our transaction. We finished the coffee. Freddy asked if I was enjoying my stay in his country. "So much," I told him, "that I'm willing to pay for the privilege of not having to leave." Freddy cracked a thin, mirthless smile and told me to return in two weeks. My new papers would be ready.

The muscleman drove me alone back into town by a different route. I knew this because we went past the Basílica de Nuestra Señora de Zapopan, something we hadn't done on the way out. Freddy obviously didn't want me to know how to get to his house on my own. The silent goon dropped me off in front of the Hotel Fenix. He hadn't spoken a single word the entire time.

Toward the end of the first week in March, I did the whole thing all over again. Drove up to Guad, met Freddy and his bodyguard at the Fenix, went with them out to his house and back, each way by a route we hadn't taken before. To brighten the day, the big thug wore a lime-green polyester leisure suit. I wondered where the hell he bought his wardrobe. Freddy and I drank coffee in his living room. He presented me with two brand-new single-entry tourist cards, dated four days earlier. Hulking in a far corner, the glowering bodyguard never took his eyes off me.

Returning this time, I sat in Bitter Lemon with the window rolled down, staring at the entrance of the Hotel Fenix. Traffic noise and black bus fumes provided an unpleasant contrast to the pristine seaside tranquillity of Barra. I figured Nick and his pals needed to meet with Freddy. They had watches to sell. He was a man who was buying.

I let an hour drift past, watching the Fenix doorman hail an occasional cab. I waited for something not likely to happen. Impossible good luck to spot Nick out of the blue, on his way to see Freddy. Why hang around waiting for a miracle? I locked the car, dropped a dos décimos, a copper twenty-centavo coin, into the meter, buying fifteen minutes of parking time, and crossed the street. The doorman maintained a distant air in his braided cap and magenta uniform, haughty as a comic opera generalissimo. I told him I wanted to see Freddy.

He gave me a look of utter disdain, saying Freddy would not be back until Monday. It was *Viernes Santo*. Mr. Freddy attended services today and would again on Easter Sunday.

"¿Y mañana?" I asked.

The doorman regarded me like something stuck to the bottom of his shoe. In Spanish slow and simple enough for a three-year-old to understand, he explained that Freddy was a very pious man who did not conduct business during *Semana Santa*.

I went into the lobby and forked over a couple pesos for copies of the Mexico City *News* and *El Occidental*, Guadalajara's daily paper. I took them into the public toilet off the lobby and settled into a pristine stall. Traveling third-class in Mexico taught me to take full advantage of my gringo status at every opportunity. I leafed through the *News* first. It was printed in English. No mention of Barra de Navidad. I went over *El Occidental* more carefully, figuring news of a murder in Jalisco would show up first in the local rag. I read enough Spanish to get the gist of things but saw nothing about Frankie in the latest edition. They probably hadn't found her body yet. That couldn't last long. Dead meat grows rank fast in the tropics.

I walked back to the van. Sticking around was a losing proposition. Maybe Nick and the gang might show up looking for Freddy. More likely, they'd already come by yesterday and got the word way before me. If they wanted to do business, they'd have to wait until Monday like everybody else. Time wasn't on my side. I was nearly flat broke and living in my van like a bum. Somebody might discover Frankie's body anytime. What if I got arrested before I located Linda? What if she was already dead? Feeling sick with my own impotence, I drove away and cruised the neighborhood until I found a street without meters. I parked, locked the VW, and strolled off with the Between the Acts tin tucked in my shirt pocket.

A long walk on a beautiful spring day. The clear blue sky free from the persistent gray exhaust pall. The holiday exodus had reduced traffic to a minimum. Jacaranda trees bloomed along the sidewalks. Masses of blue blossoms billowed overhead. Magenta bursts of bougainvillea spilled over stucco walls crowned with broken bottles, jagged shards glinting in the sunlight. All that color took my mind off the shit-pit I'd fallen into.

I strolled under rows of poinciana trees past the Teatro Degollado at the western end of the Plaza de la Liberación toward the rear of the Catedral Metropolitana, staring up at those scarlet flowers flaming against an azure sky. They promised absolution. The plaza looked deserted. An old man swept fallen leaves with a bundle of twigs. Band music played in the distance.

A procession was under way by the cathedral's front entrance. I edged into the crowd watching a Passion Play from across the Calle Alcalde. A red-cloaked Roman centurion lashed an Indian Christ stooping under the weight of an enormous wooden cross. Most of the spectators standing along the edge of the main square were local residents, holding parasols. Shoeshine boys toting elaborate brass-studded boxes prowled for customers.

I saw several middle-aged American tourists, cameras slung around their necks. Moving between them, I spotted a clean-cut young couple holding hands. They looked to be college age. His blond hair was cropped short. He sported crisp chinos and a short-sleeved white Safari shirt fresh from the laundry, showcasing his powerful arms. She was pretty in a well-scrubbed farm girl way, pink cotton summer dress, long brown hair pulled back in a ponytail. I considered avoiding them, but even straight arrows smoked weed.

"Pretty weird." I sidled up with a friendly smile.

"Completely pagan," the boy said, frowning disapproval.

I let that one pass. "Where you from?" I saw they both wore wedding rings.

"Utah," the wife said.

"We're both juniors at Brigham Young," her husband added.

It always amazed me how open Americans traveling in foreign countries were when they met someone from home. They'd tell their whole life story to a total stranger in a heartbeat. I'd done it myself with Nick.

"Been in Mexico long?" I asked.

"Only a week," he said.

"Spring break," she chirped.

Across the street, the Huichol Jesus staggered forward past a row of acolytes holding gold-embroidered banners aloft. "We've got four more days," muscle man said.

"Want to buy some smoke?" I asked.

"What?" The blond dude scowled.

"Got the best you ever tasted."

"What's he saying, honey?" The farm girl didn't have a clue.

Brigham Young grabbed me around the neck. "He's trying to sell us narcotics! Go find a cop!"

"What?"

"Get a policeman, Kathy! He's selling marijuana."

Eyes wide as a doe caught in the headlights, Kathy backed away, not exactly sure of her mission but duty-bound to do as hubby instructed. In a moment, she was lost in the crowd.

"I can't breathe," I gasped.

Mr. Clean was very strong. I felt the iron bulge of his

biceps against my larynx. He relaxed his grip a bit and I turned slightly sideways, driving my elbow full-force into his midsection. He made a sound like a tire deflating and let go. I brought my knee up hard between his legs. He doubled over with a toad-croak, and I slipped away among the onlookers. All eyes stared straight ahead at the Passion Play. I didn't run, strolling along like an innocent tourist.

Heart racing, I crossed Avenida Hidalgo into the Plaza de la Rotonda. What an idiot, trying to peddle dope to a pair of Mormons who didn't even drink Coke. Looking over my shoulder, gripped by paranoia, I walked past a ring of columns circling an eternal flame in honor of Jalisco's dead heroes. The Museo Regional de Guadalajara stood just west of the plaza, a block-long two-story colonial building, once some sort of seminary. A perfect sanctuary.

Crossing Calle Liceo, I passed horse-drawn *calandrias* waiting at the curb opposite the Plaza de la Liberación. I'd come full circle around the cathedral. No one watched me duck into the museum's main entrance. Admission was ten pesos. I hated parting with the price of a day's food, but I'd never find Linda locked up in jail.

I wandered through the several rooms devoted to pre-Columbian pottery from western Mexico until the museum opened into a central tree-shaded courtyard enclosed by arched colonnades. An empty leaf-littered fountain stood at the center.

I paused. Had I killed enough time for the coast to be clear? Across the way, I noticed two muscular long-haired gringos staring at Benito Juárez's carriage. They had the look of hippies, wearing jeans and denim work shirts, advertising their individuality with a pair of colorful vests, one Guatemalan, the other Afghan or Nepalese. These guys came on as world travelers, yet their threads were off the racks of East Village hippie emporiums.

Taking it slow and easy, I strolled across the courtyard. "Mussolini was named for Juárez," I said, stepping up beside them. "Il Duce's parents were lefties."

"No shit?" the tall guy in the Guatemalan vest said. "What's the big deal with him anyway?" I explained about Cinco de Mayo and how Juárez led the Mexican army to its unlikely victory over the French at the Battle of Puebla. How a Zapotec from Oaxaca ended up president of Mexico. How he stood Emperor Maximilian in front of a firing squad. That broke the ice and got us talking. The burly bearded one said he was called Tundra. He came from Norway. "Trondheim," he said in his pleasant singsong voice. I pressed him and he confessed his real name was Birger. The big fellow hailed from Parkersburg, West Virginia, and was named Vernon. "Call me Vern."

They asked my name. "Cisco," I told them, playing it safe with a vagabond smile. "Like the Cisco Kid."

Out on the street with my new pals, I suggested we grab a beer. We found a little place on a side street serving a full five-course soup to flan *comida corrida* for six pesos. We talked about my long stay in Mexico, two previous trips in '62 and '64. These dudes had both been here less than a month. I sounded like an old pro.

"Know where to score some weed?" Vern asked.

I grinned. "You guys just hit the jackpot."

MAÑANA

❀

We walked five or six blocks to their hotel, a former monastery where the rooms all faced an open central courtyard. Vern lived on the second floor with his plump girlfriend, Dee. Tundra had a room on the other side of the surrounding balcony. He went to get some beer, returning with six Coronas, along with Nigel and Martin, two polite young Englishmen built like rugby players.

I took a dorf from my slim cigar tin and set it aflame. The joint went hand-to-hand around the circle. The group got higher than Telstar. They all wanted to buy my product, balking only when I told them the price was a hundred pesos a lid.

"Shit, man, it's cheaper back home," Vern complained.

"I'm selling dime bags for eight bucks. *Puro* Michoacán. Absolutely clean. No twigs, stems, or seeds. You're getting twice the weight for half the price."

After more stoned grumbling they agreed to buy four lids. I left their hotel floating on "hot air." Four hundred pesos was fifty bucks. My finances had just increased nearly tenfold. It took half an hour to walk back to the car. The VW had been parked there for several hours, long enough to get noticed. I didn't want anyone watching so I got in and drove off.

Headed west to Calzada Independencia, then north to the equestrian statue of Morelos at the entrance to a little park named in his honor. I pulled over by a sloping patch of green, a quiet spot where no other cars parked. Tugging the Nido can from its hiding place, a frozen grip of panic

45

seized the back of my neck. I plucked out four plastic baggies and tossed them into a straw *bolsa*, dumping soiled clothes on top.

I needed to beef up security. Any small town traffic fuzz, the *tamarindos* in their khaki uniforms, could pull me over. A microbus was an obvious target for Mexican cops. At least Bitter Lemon sported a nondescript battleship-gray paint job, no swirling Day-Glo acid arabesques. Small advantage. I put the van in gear and cruised toward the end of the park. Passing a sequence of unfamiliar streets, I found myself back in Vern and Tundra's neighborhood. Half a block away, I saw the hotel and eased to a stop at the curb.

I climbed the age-scalloped stairs. Some unspecified doubt nagged at the back of my mind. A warning I didn't hear. Knocking on the door got no answer. I pushed and it swung slowly open, creaking on un-oiled hinges. They were all asleep. Vern and Dee on the swaybacked bed, the others slumped against the walls like campesinos at siesta time.

Vern's eyelids parted like a drowsing lizard's. "You bring it?"

Icy fear clawed at my belly. I was on my own against four big guys. What if they beat me up and took the dope? I had the Randall strapped to my belt under my untucked Hawaiian shirt but not the balls to use it. "You got the dinero?" I tried to sound noncommittal.

"On the table."

I counted the banknotes, all in twenties and fifties, and shoved them into my jeans. Vern lurched over from the bed. Taking the baggies from the *bolsa*, I set the lids side-by-side on the tabletop. Tundra staggered upright to join us. "Got more if you want it," I said. "Blotter acid, too."

"What you asking?" Tundra's torpid deliberation exaggerated his accent.

"Fifty pesos a hit."

Vern's whistle signaled his disapproval.

"We pay half," Tundra mumbled.

"Sorry, man. No can do. It's boss shit. Five hundred mics." The boys were getting surly. "Gotta split," I said. "Catch me on the plaza tomorrow if you want to score." I made for the door. Why let the vibe darken further? "Later . . ."

My lingering paranoia grew stronger going down the worn stone stairs. First day as a drug dealer. I had lots to learn. Nearly got busted on the plaza. Didn't think the whole deal through before making this delivery. In the courtyard, I spotted a trio of skinny zoot-suiters hanging around on the street outside the arched entranceway. Stopped me in my tracks. Their outdated *pachuco* outfits made them look all the more menacing. My mental state drew these three to me. Fear always attracted the demons it dreaded most.

I got a grip and saw they were just jive-ass teenagers togged out in twenty-year-old double-breasted jackets a couple sizes too large. Stay cool, I thought, heading out from the shaded protection of the courtyard into the bright blaze of day.

"¿Quieres grifa?" the tallest young tough asked, swaggering toward me. The kid looked to be about eighteen or nineteen. A faint downy mustache embroidered his upper lip.

"*¿Qué?*"

"*Grifa. ¿Quieres fumar?*" He was trying to sell me weed, asking if I'd like to smoke. His face had the angled bronze features of an Indian.

"*No gracias,*" I said. The other two hung back. They were much younger, no more than thirteen or fourteen.

"*¿Como no? Es mota muy loca.*" He said it was very crazy shit.

"*No me gusta.*" I kept a straight face when I told him I didn't like the stuff, knowing I reeked of pot.

"You lie, gringo." The aspiring bandito laughed with scorn. "I spick Ingliss. *No soy estúpido.* You a marijuanista!"

I didn't like the edge in his voice. It was time to split. "*Otra vez,*" I said, turning away and walking off in the opposite direction from my van.

The juvenile delinquent grabbed me by the shoulder. "*¿A dónde va?*" He demanded to know where I was going.

I shrugged off his grip. "*No es asunto tuyo.*" None of his fucking business.

"*No, hombre.*" He sneered at me. "*Dáme su dinero.* You money. You gimme *dinero!*"

"*¿Qué? No entiendo.*" I stalled for time, pretending not to understand. The icy grip of terror closed on my racing heart.

"*¡Dinero, pinche gringo culero!*" He was in my face now, calling me a pube and a cunt, rubbing his first finger and thumb together in the universal sign for money. "*Dáme todo.*" He wanted all of it. My brand-new bankroll.

I suppressed an impulse to take off and run. It was a bad move. Predators thrive on weakness. Better standing my ground. "*¡Cupa mi pito, chingado!*" I spat at him. Suck my dick, fucker! "*¡No soy un hombre sin huevos!*" I don't know if I got the lingo just right but telling him I was the one with balls really pissed him off.

"*¡Maricón!*" he hissed, and a switchblade flashed alive in his hand like an electric snake. "*¡Su dinero!*" He waved his dagger under my nose. "*¡Pronto!*"

"*Momentito.*" I took a step back. This was it, the moment of truth. No way I was giving my bread to this asshole. He thought I was a pussy pushover. So much the better. Always an advantage being underestimated. I reached behind as if groping for my wallet, unsnapping the keeper strap around the Randall's grip. "*¡Tomalo si puedes!*" I shouted, drawing my knife in a single swift move. Take it if you can! My assailant backed away at the sudden flash of the blade. He grinned at me, unimpressed by the shrill ring of my voice.

"*Bueno.*" He advanced, switchblade extended at arm's length. "*¡Ahora bailamos!* Now we dance."

I turned slowly right, holding the hunting knife up in front of my face. How could this be happening? In broad daylight on a public street? I didn't dare look around for passing pedestrians, my eyes locked on my opponent's venomous stare. It felt unreal. Like being in a movie. The only knife fight I'd ever seen had been on stage at the Winter Garden when I took a high school date to see *West Side Story*. Those guys were just chorus boys putting on a show. This scrawny criminal called it "dancing."

I was scared shitless and the other guy knew it. Not a good time to be stoned. He grinned at me with complete contempt as we circled each other on the sidewalk. The younger kids barked encouragement, sidling up behind me as a distraction. If I looked away from his deadly eyes for even a blink, I'd feel his shiv burning in my gut. At least we were both right-handed so no advantage either way. As if he could read my mind, the *bandito* began flipping his switchblade back and forth from hand to hand like a juggler, grinning at his display of dexterity and the unnerving effect he saw it had on me.

He feinted a jab with his left hand and I dodged to my right. In almost the same moment, he tossed the switchblade to his right hand, lunging forward and stabbing me in the shoulder. Blinding pain burned through me. I screamed, reacting with pure primal instinct as I slashed out at the two-bit hood, swinging my arm in a wild arc. The Randall caught him across the cheek, laying open his flesh easy as slicing butter. It was the *pachuco*'s turn to scream. He grabbed at his face, blood spurting between his fingers. I swung back the other way. The broad blade cut across his shirt, leaving a red line along the middle of his chest. Howling, he dropped his switchblade and took off running, two amigos close on his heels.

Exhilaration trembled through me. My high had vanished in the ice-cold clarity of primal fear. I stared at the Randall's gleaming blade, clean of any blood, and slipped the knife back into its sheath. My left shoulder pulsed with pain, every heartbeat amplified deep within the injury. There was almost no blood on my floral-patterned shirt. Only a small tear in the cloth. I reached down and picked the switchblade off the pavement. The spoils of war.

Back at Bitter Lemon, I got out the first-aid kit, the tequila bottle, and a clean shirt. I climbed into the front seat, locking all the doors. The trophy switchblade went into the glove compartment. After a couple healthy swigs to calm my nerves, I peeled off my shirt and took a look at the wound. It didn't appear to be much, a clean puncture maybe half an inch wide, oozing blood in a thin trickle. I knew it went deep into the muscle because it hurt like hell.

Using a sterile gauze pad, I wiped the wound clean and daubed on some Mercurochrome with a Q-tip. It was the alcohol-based kind I called "tiger blood" when I was a kid. It stung fiercely. I took this as a good sign. My mother always told me pain meant the disinfectant was busy doing its job killing germs. I squeezed a line of Neosporin on another gauze pad and finished the dressing with strips of adhesive tape. All things considered, I got off pretty easy.

On my way out of the city, I pulled over at a roadside *tienda* and bought five hundred grams of powdered milk weighed out into a paper sack. I asked the *patrón* for a cardboard box. All he had was the bottom half from a flat of canned goods. "*Bueno,*" I said.

I popped a Pacífico for the road and set off for Lake Chapala. Somewhere along the lonely stretch between Buenavista and Zapotitlán, I stopped and smoked a dorf. Time to relax and let go of the bad chivvy-duel vibe. Very little traffic. I unloaded the Nido can and traced an outline of its rectangular base onto the cardboard flat with a Magic Marker. My knife sliced easily through the corrugations. I thought of the *pachuco's* cheek and Frankie's throat parting under the same blade.

Forcing the cardboard square down into the Nido can on top of the bagged marijuana, I poured in the powdered milk, filling the can to just below the rim. It looked very convincing. I scattered the leftovers to the wind in a chalky cloud.

It was past six o'clock, sun setting over the lake, when I drove into Jocotepec, my van shuddering over the uneven cobblestones. I parked on the plaza, opposite the little church. Several young couples strolled modestly around the central bandstand. A dull throb in my shoulder resonated through the insulation of marijuana and booze. I walked a couple blocks toward the lakefront, looking for a place I'd heard about in Barra. The Hotel la Quinta had once been a stagecoach stop. Claimed to be the oldest operating hotels in Mexico, the sort of place celebrated in a five-dollars-a-day guide.

I didn't want a room, feeling flush not foolish. Linda and I never spent more than ten pesos a night for hotel rooms during our travels in Mexico. Toilets always down the hall. *Sin baño* became our watchword. La Quinta claimed to have a great restaurant. I sat at a two-top on the patio, facing the sunset blazing across the lake. The cool evening air felt pleasant after the heat of the day.

A waiter brought a candle flickering in a red glass bowl and set it in the center of the table. Linda would have loved this place. I remembered a rooftop restaurant in Marrakesh on the edge of the Medina with candles dancing all along the parapets. We feasted on *bastilla* and couscous, gazing down on the night world of the Place Jemaa el-Fna where crowds milled between steaming food stalls, entertained by jugglers and magicians, adolescent dancing boys costumed as girls, oud players, and bearded Berber storytellers. Our one big treat. Other evenings we ate shish kebab on the street among the djellaba-clad throng.

I recalled Linda's beautiful cameo face smiling at me through the candlelight five years ago. Wished she sat across from me now, smiling her private smile. I hoped she was safe wherever she was, convinced she'd been taken by force, a witness to Frankie's murder, kidnapped to keep her from talking.

I ordered *pescado blanco*, the house specialty, a lemon sole-flavored whitefish caught with nets only in Lake Chapala. Making small talk with the waiter to break through my loneliness, I asked if he knew someplace nearby where I could camp for the night. He told me to drive south out of town for about three miles along the lake in the direction of San Pedro Tesistán. At a straight stretch of beach close to the road, I could pull over anywhere with no questions asked.

The waiter's directions were a hole in one. I left Jocotepec in the dark. A full moon had risen and the lake shimmered in its silver light, making it easy to find the beach he mentioned. I angled off the road and parked under a cluster of palm trees, careful not to drive too far into the sand. Lighting a dorf, I went for a walk along the water's edge, hoping moonlit serenity might ease my troubles away.

Didn't work. Looking up at the moon, I saw a small shadow

crescent had taken a bite out of one side. An eclipse. Something creepy about the way a red stain slowly spread across the silver face. No wonder primitive people feared eclipses. For the next couple hours, I strolled along the shore as the moon grew redder and redder. Around eleven o'clock, I stared up at an ominous disc, rusty with dark blood. I felt condemned by heaven itself.

Back at the van, I drank more beer, washing down shots of tequila in a misguided attempt to blunt the pain. My physical injury was nothing compared to the wound in my heart. Visions of Frankie's staring waxworks eyes haunted me. What if they'd done it to Linda? Cut her throat and left her alone and cold in some *sin baño* hotel room. This kind of thinking was a dead end street, but I just couldn't shake it. Hopeless. The only word to sum things up. Hopeless . . . Hopeless . . .

I crawled into Bitter Lemon. Abandon all hope, ye who enter here. Making sure the doors were locked, I changed the dressing on my stab wound and settled down for what looked to be a sleepless night. The ceiling dome light was barely enough to read by. I wriggled under the comforter, propped-up against the back of the front seat with a pillow. Tossing aside today's papers, I came across the copy of *Zap Comix* with its bookmark sheet of blotter acid.

The pulp pages made me smile. Drawn in a goofy old-fashioned big-foot style by an artist going by the improbable name of R. Crumb, the comic reminded me of the pornographic eight-page Tijuana Bibles we passed around the Grace Church School playground. "Mr. Natural Visits the City," a story about a short bearded guru, an obvious parody of the Maharishi, made me laugh even when I read it a second time. A bitter laugh born from utter desperation. The sound of a condemned man locked away on death row where only other doomed inmates hear him howl.

HOLY
SATURDAY

I woke up remembering a page from *Zap Comix*. "Keep on truckin.'" The absurd phrase staying with me all morning like a mantra, "Keep on truckin'. . . Keep on truckin' . . ." My left shoulder felt stiff and sore. It ached when I tried to lift my arm above my head. I ignored it and brewed a pot of coffee, rustling myself up some breakfast. The ice bought in Barra was almost gone. A small chunk floated in my cooler, the meltwater cold enough to keep the beer chilled. I fried eggs and tortillas. For a brief moment, the world seemed normal. Linda was just off behind a tree taking a leak or something. I started cleaning and packing and the mood dissolved. Frankie's ghost wrapped her icy arms around me again.

Driving back to Guad, I thought about filth. I felt dirty. My armpits reeked. Pollution seeped deep into my soul. I found my first stop in the guidebook. The Baños San Martín, a public bathhouse on Cabañas sat behind the big Mercado Libertad on Independencia. For three pesos, fifty, I gained entry and received a threadbare cotton towel. A safe-deposit box was included in the admission price. I locked up my watch, wallet, and car keys. After using the toilet, I stripped down and hung my soiled clothes in a nearby locker.

I used my own soap and shampoo and shaved under the steaming spray. The hot water streamed down. I lathered myself in suds. The tepid shower in Barra had failed to wash me clean. I felt Frankie's blood corrupting my flesh and don't know how long I stood soaping myself over and over, scrubbing my skin pink. The gauze pad with its small bull's-eye of dried blood peeled off, and I used the soap to clean my wound in spite of stinging pain. Toweling dry, I sat on a wooden bench and cooled down. The stain of Mercurochrome had washed away, revealing a swollen redness around the puncture. I figured it was infected. Cleanliness was not even close to godliness. Something deep inside still smelled of rot.

I changed into the clean clothes I'd brought with me and walked out of the bathhouse into the bright midday sun. Hunger rumbled in my gut. After taping a new bandage on my shoulder at the van, I dumped my soiled clothes with the other dirty laundry, picked up the bag of trash accumulated over the past couple days and headed for the Mercado Libertad, a vast modern open-air building capped by a zigzagging cantilevered concrete roof. I read in the guidebook the market was designed ten years ago by a student who won some big architecture prize.

The place teemed with activity. I tossed my garbage in a large trash receptacle and headed for the mezzanine food stalls. The crowd was mostly housewives shopping, but I kept a sharp watch for teenage *banditos*. Who knew how big their *pachuco* gang might be. They'd be looking for a gringo in a Hawaiian shirt just like me. At a tiny *puesto* presided over by a genial Huichol grandmother sporting a bright gold front tooth, I gorged on *birria*, an oven-baked *cabrito* stew with roasted chilies, a Guadalajaran specialty. The succulent baby goat welcomed a squeeze of lime and a generous slash of the local hot sauce called *puya*.

The eastern end of the market looked out over the severe modernistic Plaza San Juan de Dios. The Calzada Independencia Sur ran along its far edge, the drab buildings across the broad boulevard sporting forty-foot neon signs on their roofs advertising Coke, 7-Up, and Corona. I found a newspaper vendor, bought a copy of *El Occidental* and sat on one of the plaza's square planters. Photos of the eclipse on the front page. The blood moon didn't look so deadly in black and white. Other headlines dealt with what Díaz Ordaz had to say on the anniversary of FDR's death and the arrest of a local *fútbol* hero for assault. I searched the articles for a report of Frankie's murder. No mention of any crime in Barra de Navidad.

It seemed impossible. How could her body not have been found? Perhaps the news had yet to reach the big city. Barra was only hours away by car or bus but might as well have existed in an alternate universe. I didn't know what to do. Hang out at the Fenix in case the gangsters might show up? Drive around the city at random all day in the off chance of spotting one of them on the street? It all seemed an exercise in futility.

I searched for a first-class *farmacia* and found a modern-looking place along Calle Pedro Moreno. The guy in the white surgical coat looked like Richard Boone on *Medic*. I unbuttoned my Hawaiian shirt and peeled back the bandage to show him my wound. He agreed there was infection, telling me not to use any more Mercurochrome. Change the dressing three times a day and continue applying Neosporin. The druggist sold me a ten-day course of penicillin. One pill twice a day before meals.

I headed next for the Centro Histórico where people went when they wanted to kill time, burning one on the drive over. After parking in the underground garage across from the cathedral, I strolled past the nineteenth-century French bandstand at the center of the Plaza de Armas, an ironwork echo of New Orleans. People milled. Not enough to make a crowd.

In a flash, I saw Shank, dressed all in black. Had on his knitted watch cap. The little man headed across the plaza in the direction of the government palace. My heart skipped a beat as I set out after him. I didn't run or call his name, stealth being always prudent when stalking dangerous animals. I walked at a very fast clip, weaving among the torpid tourists at warp speed.

Ten paces behind the man in black, I broke into a sprint. I knew he packed a knife. Didn't want that curved linoleum-cutter slicing through my guts.

"Hey, Shank!" I yelled, sliding to a stop five feet in front of him. A short Mexican man with a thick black mustache stared at me in confusion.

"*¿Dígame?*" The bewildered stranger asked.

"*Lo siento, señor,*" I said, backing away, flashing my awkward smile. "*Me equivoqué.*"

Smoking reefer enhanced the chances of mistaken identity, a lesson learned five years ago in Morocco. Stoned on hash in Marrakech, Linda and I went out on the Jemaa el-Fna one night searching for something to eat. She spotted a large enamel bowl in one of the stalls, filled with what we took to be her mother's famed spinach soufflé. Seated on the bench, I noticed all the other customers came from the dregs of society, legless beggars wearing rags. Gaunt men missing eyes and fingers. It had to be the cheapest place in town.

They glared at us as the "chef" ladled-out two small bowls of swill tasting like lawnmower clippings soaked in kerosene. Forcing a big smile, I said something in clumsy French about how delicious it was. The scum of the earth glared with hostility. Linda pushed her bowl my way, saying she'd puke if she took another bite. I ate hers, too, smiling all the while.

Smiling that same sick smile, I hurried off, escaping from the *mexicano* I'd just called Shank. Bad luck if it meant something really nasty in Spanish. I sought refuge in the eighteenth-century Palacio del Gobierno. It was almost siesta and the Jalisco state capital building was closing. I left and headed toward the Teatro Degallado, wondering what to do. The museums were also closing. No point in hanging around.

"Cisco!" a voice behind me called. It was one of the Brits. I couldn't remember which one.

We walked into the Plaza de la Liberación and found a private place to sit in the shade of a flamboyant tree. The Brit and his pals wanted more mota. "And some acid, too, like you said," Martin/Nigel stammered. "We'd sort of like to buy some weight. Three pounds, maybe."

I did a quick mental calculation. "Fifty lids'll give you three, plus a couple ounces left over."

"Can't you cut us a deal if we buy that much?"

"No deals. Fifty lids. Five thousand pesos."

"So. Five thousand is like what? Three hundred dollars?"

"Four hundred," I said, getting up to leave. Easy to talk tough when I wasn't outnumbered. "I'll throw in some free acid if you're interested. Otherwise, don't waste my time."

"Okay . . ." The Brit sounded doubtful. "When do we meet up?"

I felt a pang of fear. No way I'm carrying three pounds of weed, all alone, into their hotel room. I might get jumped. And maybe those *pachucos* were still hanging around outside. Not the fall guy anymore. "Here's what we're gonna do," I said.

"Remember the straw *bolsa* I came with yesterday? Had colored stripes? You can buy one at the main market for about five pesos. Fill it with a couple dozen oranges."

"You're not making sense, mate."

"Pay attention. I'll meet you in Morelos Park. Know where that is?" The Englishman shook his head. "Get a map. It's about six blocks from your hotel. I'll be there at four with the shit. At a bench near the bandstand. Come alone. Just you. And bring the sack of oranges. At five o'clock, I'm leaving." I looked at my watch. "You've got three hours to get it together." I started walking toward the Grecian portico of the Teatro Degollado.

"*¿Parque Morelos?*" Brit-boy called after me, experimenting with his Spanish.

"*Sí,*" I answered. "*A las cuatro de la tarde.* I'll wait an hour."

I cut over to the Plaza de los Laureles opposite the cathedral entrance. Half an hour remained on my meter in the basement garage. I hated wasting those few precious centavos. Driving down Juárez to Independencia, I found my way back to the Mercado Libertad and went in search of oranges.

All the butcher shops stood shuttered tight, but many fruit and vegetables stalls didn't close during siesta. Cries of "*un-peso-un-peso-un-peso,*" and "*mas barata . . . mas barata . . .*" echoed around me as I passed between rows of gleaming produce. Oranges proved a common commodity. A bargaining war sprang up between rival sellers. I bought a dozen from each, hauled the fruit back to the van in my striped *bolsa*. Two hours to kill before taking care of business.

I drove out on the Chapala road, turning onto a dirt lane

halfway to the summit. After pouring the powdered milk into a plastic bowl, I layered fifty lids on the bottom of the straw *bolsa*, covering the weed with a folded newspaper and heaping oranges on top. When the powder went back in, the Nido can appeared to be only half-full. I hoped it looked more deceptive that way.

Impossible to feel mellow. I thought of Linda, tied-up in the trunk of the Firebird or lying in some godforsaken ditch with her throat cut. Figuring it was time to start my penicillin regimen, I swallowed a pill and opened a can of tuna fish. I ate straight from the tin with a spoon. Everything tastes great when you're high. Before leaving, I remembered the promised acid and snipped the top row off the blotter paper with our sewing kit scissors. I folded the six doses one on top of the other concertina-fashion and slipped the little packet into my wallet.

At twenty minutes before the hour, I drove back into the city, arriving in the park about 4:05 p.m. I sauntered under the trees carrying my bulging *bolsa*, found an empty bench, and waited. I should have brought a book. Instead, I sat there watching the world go by, marking time by the steady pulse in my injured shoulder. By quarter to five, I had about given up when I spotted the Brit moving briskly through the park, looking in every direction, panic etched on his face. He carried a striped straw *bolsa* full of oranges.

He saw me at last and came over, sitting down on the other end of the bench to catch his breath. He acted like we were strangers. First cool thing he'd done.

"Nice to see you, Martin," I said after a couple minutes.

"Uhm . . . it's Nigel, actually. . . ."

"You bring the dinero?"

Nigel slid closer on the bench and handed me a wad of cash, all in hundreds, bound with a rubber band. I thumbed through, counting fifty. "*Bueno,*" I said, shoving the money into my pocket and sliding my orange-filled sack toward Nigel with my foot. "Check it out. Be discreet. Dump the oranges into your sack."

Nigel followed instructions, handing me his *bolsa*, heavy with fruit. I watched as he lifted the newspaper and started his tally. "There's white powder on them," he said.

"Not what you think."

"Looks good," he said, smoothing today's *El Occidental* back into place.

I gathered oranges out of my *bolsa*, two at a time, dropping them into his until they camouflaged the stash. "Here." I pulled the folded blotter acid from my wallet. "Six hits. Cut 'em apart at the fold."

"Thanks, man."

I got to my feet, picking up Nigel's new *bolsa*, and walked away.

"See you around, Cisco," Nigel called after me.

Not fucking likely, I thought. "*Hasta la vista,*" I said, never looking back.

It grew dark as I drove again toward Lake Chapala. I had six hundred pesos from the bankroll in my pocket. The rest remained hidden in a little compartment I'd rigged behind the dashboard for a small traveling stash. Why wasn't feeling flush the same as feeling good? I set fire to a fat one and rolled down the windows. By the time I pulled into Jocotepec, I felt only the persistent ache in my soul. I headed straight to Hotel La Quinta, parking out front. Before locking the van, I sprayed the interior with a can of Glade brought from Frisco. Playing it safe, I gave my hair and shirt a quick shot.

A chill breeze pierced the night air. I bypassed the patio, taking a table in the dining room against the back wall. The polished floor shone in the candlelight. I had the same waiter and ordered the same meal. After the *pescado blanco*, I sipped a second *cerveza* and took my penicillin. Clearing the table, the waiter asked if I'd found a nice place to camp last night.

"*Sí*," I said, "*muy bonito.*"

Lake Chapala came from the tears of ancient gods, the waiter explained, pointing through the open doors across the patio to the first glimmer of moonrise silvering the dark water. When he brought the bill, he asked if I would return to the same spot tonight.

"*¿Cómo no?*"

Driving out of town, moonlight made my headlamps superfluous. The luminous glow on the surface of Chapala had me dreaming about a lake of tears. My own grief could fill an ocean with sorrow.

Linda loved the moon, enchanted by its cool ethereal light. All phases delighted her from the first grinning crescent to a watermelon slice at the quarter and the off-balance tilted gibbous. She felt happiest when it was full. Linda called herself a true lunatic. She once told me not to be corny and look for the face of a man in the moon. "Turn your head sideways," she said. "You'll see a rabbit running. That's how they see it in Indonesia."

I wished we were together tonight in far-off Indonesia. Wherever Linda was, I hoped she was safe. Maybe she ran out on me because I killed Frankie. Or thought I did. Even if I never saw her again, I wanted her to be alive.

The moon glimmered on the lake as I pulled in under the palms. I set to work organizing things, my mind a blank, shutting the door on reality one more time. I tugged on a sweater and poured what was left of my cheap tequila into a tin cup, squeezing in half a lime to cut its rotgut finish. Draining my drink, I lit a dorf, popped the cap on a cold Pacífico, and set off down the lakeshore. I looked up at the rabbit leaping sideways across the moon, thinking of my wife. She should be holding my hand. Laughing in the magical light. No matter how cold the wind, Linda would have insisted on skinny-dipping in the moon-bright lake, splashing handfuls of quicksilver high into the night sky. Afterward, she'd want to make love, our bodies awash in lunar radiance. Let it go, I told myself. Memories can't bring her back.

At the van, I brushed my teeth and stripped for bed. After changing the bandage on my shoulder, I locked the doors and closed the little blue corduroy curtains Linda had sewn. I crawled under the comforter, hugging the extra pillow against my chest, and slipped into a half-sleep dream filled with visions of Linda. Her freckle-sprinkled face and wavy ginger hair.

Breasts firm and sweet as ripe pears. Nipples that matched the pale rose tint of her lips. She apologized the first time we made love. "Sorry my breasts are so small," she said, studying me with wide peridot eyes. I told her they were perfect, cupping one under my hand, feeling its quickening pulse.

Linda stopped shaving under her arms last September after we arrived in Mexico. Running my tongue through the silken growth in her armpits electrified me. I loved her smooth velvet skin, the patch of apricot floss between her legs, her pliant enfolding limbs, the moist soft entry. Drifting off to sleep, I ran my hand over the pelt on my groin, remembering.

A strange sound yanked me out of my dream. Wide-awake, I heard noises inches from my head. It wasn't the wind. I opened the side curtain a crack. A group of campesinos surrounded the van. Several held flashlights, bright beams darting. They all carried machetes. After a whispered consultation with an older man, one stepped forward and inserted the tip of his blade into the narrow gap between the sliding side door and the VW's frame. I stared at the top of his head as he began forcing the lock.

In an instant, I scrambled bare-ass through the front curtains, tumbling into the driver's seat. The keys hung from the ignition. I fumbled for them in the dark and they fell to the floor. An angry face appeared at the passenger-side window, shouting incoherently. He started pounding on the glass with the butt of his machete. I groped for my keys. The window cracked like a sheet of ice. A spiderweb of fissures ran through the glass. My fingers found the key ring. I heard them all yelling, howling like a wolf pack outside. Somehow, I got the key back in the ignition and revved the engine. Jamming the van into reverse, I swerved wildly in the sand backing for the road. The rear curtains were closed. I drove blind. The bandito ran alongside, hanging onto the door handle.

The rest of them pounded on the side panels as I gained the paved road. The guy at the window glared at me when I switched on the headlights, his face a furious mask distorted through prisms of fragmented glass. "*¡Chinga tu madre!*" I screamed at him, shifting into first.

He ran faster and faster, holding tight to the door handle. I picked up speed. In the end, I dragged him down the highway. He let go when the speedometer hit twenty-five miles per hour. I saw him in my side-view mirror, tumbling like an acrobatic clown along the moonlit road.

I drove naked past the Jocotepec turnoff, heading up Highway 15 toward Guadalajara. My heart raced. Linda would have loved it. Roller coasters were her preferred mode of transportation. She never heard a dare she wouldn't take. We spent the spring and summer of '63 in Morocco and Spain. Linda sold her sporty green Triumph to bankroll the trip.

In Formentera, smallest of the Balearic Islands, we rented a farmhouse with a view of the Mediterranean for six hundred pesetas, about twelve bucks a month. Franco still ruled the roost twenty-two years after overthrowing the Loyalists. The Guardia Civil enforced his Fascist laws in their patent-leather tricorne hats. It was illegal for a woman to wear a bikini or any other two-piece bathing suit. When a Guardia told this to Linda on Playa de la Malagueta in Málaga, she asked him which piece he'd like her to remove.

Thumbing our noses at the law, we swam nude in Formentera. Only two Guardia were stationed on the island. Their main assignment seemed to be looking for naked foreigners through their binoculars. They had only bicycles for transportation like the rest of us, crude Spanish bikes without gears, lights, or hand brakes.

Linda and I pedaled out along meandering goat paths to the far reaches of the Cap de Berbería searching for safe places to swim. No beaches here, only small coves accessible by climbing down steep cliffs. One spot clogged with a haystack pile of dried seaweed provided dubious itchy comfort. We avoided the place, often crowded with German and Swedish sunbathers.

One afternoon standing on the brink of a sixty-foot cliff too steep to climb, Linda smiled at me and said, "Care for a swim?" She stripped off her blouse and shorts.

"You're crazy," I said. No denying the challenge sparkling in her chartreuse eyes. Moments later, I stood naked beside her, wondering if we'd make it down without falling or how we'd ever climb back up.

She took my hand and said, "Let's jump together."

"I don't think so," I stammered. The water looked a long way down, waves crashing against jagged rocks. A deep foaming pool half the size of a tennis court provided the only safe spot between upsurges of raging surf.

"Come on." Linda pulled me closer to the edge. "I'll count to three." Before I could protest again, I was hurtling feet-first toward the sea, hand-in-hand with my gleeful laughing wife.

Twenty miles from Jocotepec, I was out in open country half-way to Guad. I hadn't seen a light in five minutes and pulled onto a barren field. I climbed inside the sleeping compartment, drawing my curtains tightly closed. Lying in the dark, I felt certain the waiter at La Quinta sold me out. He told me where to camp in the first place. But paranoia never proved anything. Parked in the same remote spot two nights in a row. Anyone could have seen me. Bitter Lemon might be just a piece of junk back in the States, but down here, south of disorder, it was another story.

Out on the high lonesome smack-dab in the middle of remote rural nothingness, I felt like a sitting duck for sure. Alone meant vulnerable. I reached over the front seat and pulled the Randall off my belt. Back under the covers clutching the sheathed blade, I knew the outcome of my first knife fight had been pure dumb luck. Holding off a bunch of machete-armed banditos like Jim Bowie seemed a joke even if my weapon had tasted blood twice. Not remembering if you committed murder isn't much help when it comes to imagining future killings. I slept with the Randall at my side, a talisman to keep me safe.

EASTER
SUNDAY

—— • ● • ——

I awoke long before sunrise. Wearing only jeans, I stepped outside for a piss and a look around, slipping the Randall back
onto my belt. It was the perfect spot. Not a house in sight. Far
enough off the highway to avoid the headlights of passing cars.
I got my gear out from under the sleeping platform. Soon, a
pot of coffee perked on the Coleman. Last night's misadven-
ture kept me on the alert for unexpected strangers. It was *Pas-
cua*. After changing the gauze dressing and shaving, I put on

my gaudiest Hawaiian shirt for the occasion. The area around the stab wound looked a lot less red. Maybe this was wishful thinking.

A crimson sun rose to my right as I drove into the city around 6:00 a.m. The shattered passenger window turned to stained glass in its glow. I swung west on Niños Héroes, taking it all the way to Independencia. Passing the Mercado Libertad, I continued for another ten blocks on Javier Mina, looking for the Mercado El Baratillo. Linda and I shopped there four years ago. Vague memories of its location remained. A street market operating only on Sundays, it was best early in the morning before the first celebration of Mass. Everything got picked over by then.

I spotted the gathering crowd a couple blocks ahead and turned onto a side street, parking beside Muebles Hernández, a furniture store with its name painted in cursive script across the corrugated surface of a locked rolling shutter. The lakeside campesino attack on top of my *pachuco* knife fight had me thinking about protection. I needed an imposing weapon.

Peeling five hundred pesos off my bankroll, I returned the rest to its hiding place under the dash, locked up, and strolled around the corner into the sprawling street market throng. El Baratillo spread across a twenty-block area like an enormous swap meet. I pushed past groups of men eying displays of rusted tools and secondhand furniture. Women lingered around used clothing and cooking stuff. Most of them dressed in their Sunday best for church later on. Tourists checked out antiques and exotic animals. My quest made me cautious and I scanned the crowd for any teenage *pachucos* intent on revenge.

I came across a fellow with a number of old percussion revolvers arranged on a blanket spread across the sidewalk. These antique cap-and-ball pistols looked formidable. I tried to picture myself pointing one at an intruder and acting tough. Yosemite Sam came to mind. Anyone handy with firearms would know the old hogleg wasn't loaded.

Something caught my eye as I wandered past acres of tarnished silverplate. Laid out on a table among several ormolu mantel clocks, a double-barreled shotgun declared its lethal authority like a cobra lurking in a flowerbed. It was an old twelve-bore side-hammer with a pistol grip stock. I knew something about shotguns from when I was a kid. My mother had an uncle with a dairy farm upstate in the Catskills. The last couple years before he died, Dad took me bird hunting there during the fall. He gave me a little .410 single-shot and taught me to use it. I never brought down a grouse but loved popping away as they thundered out of the laurel thickets.

The old side-by-side looked pretty beat up. A lean white-haired man squinted at me. He wore a suit vest with no tie or jacket, his gray-striped shirt buttoned all the way to the collar. The weapon was marked E. M. REILLY & CO., LONDON. I opened the action, peering up through the twin barrels at the sky. The bores were badly pitted. I closed it up. The box lock felt tight for its age. Thumbing back the hammers, I dry-fired, pulling each of the double triggers. The piece had a crisp snap.

"*Es una escopeta muy fina,*" the white-haired man said, launching into his pitch. "*Fabricada en Inglaterra.*" He told me his fine shotgun was made in England.

I said nothing, not wanting to praise his gun before we

started bargaining. When I dry-fired a second time, I noted the lightness of the pull. Almost hair-triggers.

"*¿Cuánto cuesta?*" I asked. How much?

"*Mil quinientos.*"

"*Cara,*" I said, setting down the shotgun. Steep. No way I was paying fifteen hundred pesos.

"*No. Es muy barata.*" The vendor held up his hands in a gesture of helplessness. "Sheep," he said, straining to find some English. "Wary, wary sheep."

I said the shotgun was *vieja*, stressing the word for old as a pejorative. I pointed to the cracked stock. "*Rota.*"

The white-haired man ignored my objections. "Hokay," he said, using most of the English he knew. "How much for you?"

"*Cien pesos. Nada más.*" I offered a hundred pesos as my bottom line.

The man scratched his head to show he was thinking things over.

"*Mil pesos.*" Only a thousand now.

"*Ciento cincuenta,*" I fired back. The old man came down five hundred pesos. I upped my bid by fifty.

"*No.*" The vendor folded his arms defiantly across his chest. "*Imposible.*"

"*Bueno,*" I said. "*Adiós.*" I walked away. Bargaining always reached a point where you had to risk blowing the deal. It was a bluffer's game.

"*¡Cuatrocientos!*" he called after me. "*¡Trescientos!*" I kept walking. "*¡Doscientos cincuenta!*" This was his last offer. Two hundred fifty pesos wasn't bad. A fraction of the starting price. I could afford twenty bucks.

"*¡Trato hecho!*" I said. It's a deal. The white-haired man grinned as I walked back. He enjoyed bluffing as much as me. Maybe more.

"*Compañero,*" the vendor said, his smile revealing several missing front teeth. "*Regateas cómo un mexicano.*"

"*Gracias,*" I replied, digging into my jeans. "*Es un cumplido grande.*" This wasn't just bullshit on my part. Telling a gringo he bargained like a Mexican was a true compliment.

"*A su servicio.*"

I peeled three hundred-peso notes off my bankroll and gave them to the old man. He smoothed the bills out on the tabletop, one at a time, smiling all the while. "*Exacto,*" he said, placing the money in a small black tin cashbox. He extracted my change, two bright newly minted silver twenty-five-peso Olympic coins the size of Morgan dollars.

I strolled off into the crowd carrying the shotgun angled in the crook of my elbow, action open, and studied the beautiful coins. An Aztec ballplayer crouched above the Olympic rings. The symbol of Mexico, an eagle holding a rattlesnake in its talons and beak, appeared on the reverse. It was the first time I'd seen any of these. I decided to keep one for good luck. I needed all I could get.

I stashed the big side-hammer in the van's storage compartment and drove to the Mercado Libertad, parking on Cabañas. Walking among the early-morning food shoppers felt completely surreal. Three days ago, I woke up in bed next to a dead whore. Maybe I cut her throat. My wife was gone. Maybe she was the hostage of three junkie criminals. That was my best hope. It seemed absurd. How would I ever find her? Where was I supposed to look?

My only chance depended on her still being in Guadalajara. I didn't know where to start and eliminated the obvious choices. No way in hell Linda would go to Easter Mass. Same went for Nick, Doc, and Shank. I erased the cathedral from my mental list. The museums would all be closed for *Pasqua*. I pondered this while sipping a tall glass of freshly squeezed orange juice, imagining the places Linda might want to go. A lazy Sunday morning invited music. My wife dug mariachis. I liked them, too, and guessed she'd enjoy sitting at an outdoor café on the *plazuela* facing the Iglesia de San Juan de Dios, drinking a cold beer and listening to one band after the other.

I bought copies of the Mexico City *News* and *El Occidental* at the newsstand. The local English-language rags concerned themselves with neighborhood events instead of real news. Two were free. I picked up copies and shelled out a peso for *The Colony News*. Around eleven, I strolled into the mariachi plaza beside the Iglesia de San Juan de Dios and found an umbrella-shaded table in front of a pleasant café. Everything looked quiet. No sign of Linda or the others. I noticed several bands lounging under the surrounding arches in their silver-studded charro outfits and big sombreros. When a waiter approached, I ordered a *café con leche* and churros.

I read the papers, dipping a hot churro into my coffee, searching for any mention of Frankie. Nothing. Not a single line. By my second cup, I was into the local English weeklies, mostly expat gossip. I skimmed reports of flower shows, weddings, and charity luncheons. An ad in Spanish for *"una gran corrida de toros de feria"* caught my eye. Why would *The Colony News* advertise bullfights? This blood sport holdover from the ancient Roman arenas sounded like just the place to find macho guys like Shank and Nick. A long shot, but I planned on being at the bullring that afternoon.

A notice for last night's boxing matches at the Arena Coliseo on Calle Medrano grabbed my attention. The pugilism took place every Saturday night. Missed the boat on that one. Prizefights were just the ticket for tough junky ex-cons. I should have been there, checking out the fans at ringside, looking for familiar faces. Too busy selling dope. Go easy on yourself, I thought. I needed the bread if I wanted to buy tickets.

Below the boxing announcement was one for Sunday wrestling at the same venue. This triggered a flashback. I paged through *El Occidental* and found a two-column ad.

HOY!
Lucha Libra
ARENA COLISEO
Domingo 14 de abril
5:45 p.m.
Lucha en Jaula
-8- Mascaras en Juego -8-

Among the eight masked supermen were "Kid Atomica, El Gallito, Infierno, and Tigre Blanco." I wondered if watching fat masked Mexicans tossing one another around held the same attraction for second-rate crooks as blood spraying across the ring. Mexican free wrestling struck me as pretty camp. Maybe things looked different through junky eyes.

At the back of another freebie, *Spotlight on Guadalajara*, I stumbled across a small notice holding the same promise as boxing. Cockfights at noon today and again tonight at the Plaza de Gallos on the Calzada Revolución. *Peleas de gallos* provided a blood sport attractive to the dregs of society. The bottom of the barrel seemed the right place to look for Shank, Doc, and Nick. The twelve o'clock fights were already under way. I figured it was too early for the gangsters to be up and stirring, unless staggering around for their first fix of the day.

The waiter brought another *café con leche*, asking if I wanted lunch. I ordered a bowl of posole. Thick with hominy and chunks of pork and chicken, the rich soup came topped with slices of avocado and accompanied by a napkin-covered plate of warm tortillas. I washed down my penicillin pill in a swallow of coffee. If I didn't spot the gang at the bullring, I'd search them out at the Lucha Libra or the cockfights, long shots for sure. Looking for a needle in a haystack? Better pick the right haystack.

A group of mariachis in flashy green suits surrounded the table. Any tourist sitting alone must be in need of music. After launching into a few bars of "Guadalajara," a song popular with gringos, they paused. The trumpet player asked if I cared to hear a favorite tune. The price was ten pesos. "Okay," I said, "'Yo Soy el Aventurero.'"

I'd always fancied myself an adventurer and this my theme song. The band kicked off the rollicking tune. I wondered if I wasn't over my head with adventure. The song concerned the many women loved by the singer whose soul was a "bohemian troubadour." What kind of amoral monster was I? Daydreaming about make-believe romance when my wife was the prisoner of thugs. Maybe I did cut Frankie's throat. Cared so little about it even the memory meant nothing to me.

The mariachis finished their song. They stood around waiting for another request. I paid them and asked the waiter for my check. The musicians wandered off. I took care of the bill, leaving a nice tip, and split.

Buying the bullfight ticket in advance struck me as a smart move. I cut across the Plaza San Juan de Dios to the Plaza de Toros Progresso and found a short line by the ticket windows. When I got to the *Sombra General* window, I asked for the cheapest ticket on the shady side. The guy spotted me as a gringo right away, slowing his Spanish to an idiot's pace. Today, only *novilleros* at the Progreso. These were apprentice bullfighters who had not yet participated in the *alternativa* ceremony elevating them to the status of *matador de toros*. The true *"espectáculo de primera calidad"* with the best professional toreros was out at the new bullring, the magnificent Plaza Monumental.

I said I didn't know about any new bullring. He told me it had been built last year, north on Independencia, *"un edificio muy espectacular."* With this guy everything was spectacular. I said I wanted to watch the novilleros and paid *ocho* pesos for my ticket. Now, I had two bullfights to attend. After that, wrestling and the roosters. A big day for sports fans.

I had more than an hour before the start of the corrida and figured on finding a place to spend the night. No more camping on the shores of Lake Chapala. Parking by the side of the road didn't seem like such a hot idea, either. On the drive into the city, I'd seen several trailer parks along the outskirts. It took fifteen minutes to walk to the van and drive out Niños Héroes to the Mexico City highway. Along the way, I stopped at a *tienda* and bought a bottle of top-shelf Herrdura Reposado tequila.

The Paradise and El Cortijo, trailer parks closest to town, were both full. I drove another six miles south to Rancho Santa Elena. For ten pesos a day, they offered toilets, showers, a laundry room, and electrical hook-ups. I said I didn't need the *"conexiones modernes."* The proprietor replied that the price remained the same. I paid in advance. Every numbered space came with a concrete patio. I was number thirty-nine.

I checked out my spot. It seemed okay, not too far from the bathhouse. Poking around for stuff in the car on a crowded street is never a smart idea. I took advantage of the privacy and dug Linda's 10X bird-watching binoculars out from under the sleeping platform. My wife treasured her Lietz Trinovid, a gift from her father, an austere man whose love of ornithology was the only pastime he shared with his daughter.

Why didn't Linda take her binoculars with her? She must have left Barra in a great hurry. Probably under duress. The secondhand gangsters gave her only enough time to gather her clothes before rushing her to the bank. Forced her to withdraw all our money. Sudden dread seized me. She must be dead.

MAÑANA

If they killed Frankie nothing would stop them from killing Linda.

Back in Guad, I couldn't find a parking spot near the Plaza de Toros Progresso and left the van many blocks away. It was past four by the time I got to the bullring. I heard the brass band playing a paso doble as I climbed the stairs to the top tier. Even in the shade, the glare of sunshine dazzled on the arena below where the *paseo*, a ceremonial entrance of the bullfighters, came to an end. I used the binoculars, scanning rows of spectators on the sunny side across the little stadium. Numbers of vacant seats declared themselves like missing teeth.

The ten-power magnification brought distant faces clearly into focus. The first of six bulls scheduled to die that afternoon galloped snorting into the ring. I moved my gaze across the mostly Mexican families in a slow sweep. Dark-skinned Nick might evade my scrutiny. I guessed he'd be with Linda. She'd stand out like an orchid in a field of sunflowers. I glassed the stands throughout the sorry business with the picadors, big fat guys lancing the bull from horseback. Working section by section, I constantly moved my position to find better angles. I came up empty-handed every time. Frustrating, futile work. The odds weren't in my favor. Hope always bets against the house.

After a few minutes, I'd scrutinized everyone on the other side. Down on the sand, a young bullfighter, called a *banderillero*, pirouetted like a ballet dancer, sunlight glinting off his sequined suit of lights as he placed the first pair of sticks, jabbing the beribboned harpoons into the bull's withers. The

81

novice matador looked on from behind the safety of the chest-high wooden fence encircling the arena. He would have to kill this bull soon and studied the animal's every move.

I ducked out the arched entryway and hurried down to street level. A familiar numb ache of futility gripped me as I walked halfway around the Plaza de Toros Progresso to the entrance marked SOL GENERAL. The gatekeeper tried to send me back. Told me I'd paid for a seat in the shade. "*Mejor,*" he said.

I climbed the stairs to the amphitheater's top tier, hearing the echoing shouts of the crowd. Every barbaric "*¡Olé!*" stabbed at my heart. Another savage taunt. I sympathized with the bewildered young bull charging around the ring in anger, unaware of the larger drama in which he was only a pawn. The doomed animal's desperate predicament mirrored my own.

I stepped out onto the aisle encircling the top row of seats. The final act, called the *tercio de muerte,* was under way. The novice matador's *faena,* an ultimate dance of death, had the audience cheering his every move. Sword in his right hand, the novillero worked the bleeding bull with the *muleta,* a small bit of red flannel cloth on a stick held in his left, guiding the animal past his body in the arcing pass called a natural. "*¡Olé!*" the crowd screamed in unison.

I had no interest in the action. I came only to scope out the spectators. Working row by row, I checked every face in the crowd without any luck. Repeated *olés* encouraged the novillero's performance. I paid no attention, trying by pure force of will to find someone I recognized.

A chorus of jeers and boos brought me out of futile concentration. I let the binoculars dangle from my neck and glanced at the arena. The novillero's kill was not going well. One of the matador's team dragged his heavy cape across the bull's flank, over and over, in an effort to work the protruding curved sword free from where the novillero had ineptly thrust it. Angry booing continued without pause, matching my mood.

I didn't stick around. The novillero would try again, perhaps again and again and again, jeered by the crowd, until either the bull was dead or his time ran out and docile steers would be led into the arena to pacify the injured animal and guide it to the slaughterhouse. I didn't want to see that ultimate disgrace or watch the goring of a clumsy bullfighter. Hurrying out the portal, I raced down the stairs to the street.

On the walk back to Bitter Lemon, I fought off feelings of frustration and failure. How impossible, looking for four people in a big city. The odds were a million to one against me. I drove north on Independencia until I spotted the hulking Plaza Monumental off to the right. It was enormous. You couldn't miss it. I must have seen it while cruising up the broad boulevard to burn a dorf. Surrounded by acres of asphalt car lot, the new bullring rose like a concrete volcano above an ocean of parked automobiles.

Large colorful posters flanked the ticket windows, listing the names of the three illustrious matadors appearing here today. I bought the cheapest general admission ticket for both *sol* and *sombra*, asking the second vendor how many people the plaza held.

"*Dieciséis mil*," he said.

Sixteen thousand might as well have been sixteen million. I had to look at every face. The picadors were at work in the second or third fight when I emerged into the sunlight high above them. A spiraling concrete sunscreen curled around the top of the arena like twisted gift ribbon on a hatbox. I spent another hour glassing the distant faces. My numb heart wasn't in it anymore. I needed a lucky break. I left the Plaza Monumental around six thirty at the start of the final bullfight, having had no success. My luck all ran out back in Barra.

The masked wrestling had begun a half-hour earlier. I needed a break from the spyglass and drove south down Independencia to the Nuevo Léon restaurant. Time to eat and take my penicillin. A *cabrito* roasted on a spit in the front window, flames dancing brighter than an advertisement for the lowest circle of hell. Just the place for me. An unseen jukebox blared over the buzz of conversation. The familiar tune nagged at my subconscious, "*pasemos la noche juntos*," echoing over and over in memory. It was the Spanish cover of "Let's Spend the Night Together," the flip side of "Ruby Tuesday," last year's number one Stone's hit. A bad-ass song that uptight radio stations back home refused to play.

I ordered *paleta*, the shoulder cut of *cabrito al pastor*, and a bottle of Pacífico. The savory mesquite-barbecued goat came with guacamole, *pico de gallo*, and a stack of warm tortillas. I was famished, wolfing down everything on my plate. Somehow when all else seems lost, a good meal provides glimmers of hope. Draining my beer, I stood and placed a *veinte* on the table under the empty bottle, enough to cover my meal plus a four-peso tip.

Glancing around the crowded restaurant, I spotted pious church-going Freddy of the Fenix huddled over coffee at a table in the rear with two other shady characters. He looked impeccably tailored as always. Maybe he'd gone to Mass this morning. His companions were a skinny guy with dark lupine features wearing a brown leather coat and a pockmarked Asian in a silver-gray Nehru jacket. I saw no sign of the heavyweight bodyguard but figured he had to be around someplace. Sure enough, a quick survey found him keeping an eye on things in his pink leisure suit, alone at a table in the far corner.

An unexpected opportunity. A chance to pick up some information about the secondhand gangsters. I walked over and stood before the ill-assorted trio. *"Con su permiso,"* I said when Freddy glanced my way. "Might I have a moment, *por favor?"*

"¡Lárgase, gringo!" wolf-face growled, telling me to beat it. I stood my ground and he rose, getting right in my space. "When gentlemen conduct private business," he hissed, "strangers are not welcome." Some trace of a foreign accent corroded his perfect English.

"I have business with Señor Freddy," I said, not giving an inch. Easy acting tough in a crowded restaurant.

"How you like I rip your fucking tongue out of your big fat mouth, *coño?"* I didn't doubt he meant every word. Figured it was time to make myself scarce.

Freddy patted the wolfman on his arm. *"Relajase, amigo,"* he said. *"No importa."*

"Este joven no tiene respeto." He told Freddy I had no respect. "Let me teach him proper manners." This last remark was directed at me.

"Sientese, compadre." Freddy tapped the seat of his companion's empty chair. *"No prestar atención a esta chinche."*

Hearing me dismissed as a bedbug seemed to calm the werewolf in the leather coat and he sat back down, glaring at me the whole time. Got the feeling he might jump up suddenly and sink his fangs into my throat. Freddy looked straight at me. "If you want more paperwork, see me in the morning," he said, turning away.

"It's not that," I blurted. "This is more important."

Freddy swiveled back. His look told me not to waste his time. "How may I be of service?" he asked.

"A word in private?"

"Habla español," the sinister Asian grumbled.

"Es bueno, Señor Chang," Freddy murmured. Turning his expressionless gaze back on me, he said, "I have no secrets from my associates. Anything you say to me is for their ears also."

"I might have a car for sale," I said.

Freddy suppressed a smile. "So many cars *might* be for sale. *¿Manaña quizás?*"

He didn't mention Nick or anyone else, but I knew at that moment they'd already talked to him about selling the Firebird, "perhaps tomorrow." Freddy turned to his companions. "This youth has an automobile for sale. You are both welcome to make an offer." He repeated it in Spanish.

The Asian looked insulted. "I did not come here to trade in automobiles." He spoke Spanish to Freddy.

"No disrespect intended, Mr. Chang," Freddy replied in Spanish. "This is a matter of no importance to you." His look told me to get lost. Freddy launched into a couple brief bursts of some birdsong lingo. The cobra in the Nehru coat nodded.

I knew it was time to go and said, "Cars are not as good business as watches? *¿Cómo no?*"

Freddy's smirk broadened into a smile. "*Sí,*" he said as if it were a joke we shared. "Watches are very good business. You also have watches for sale?"

"Not so nice as the others."

"I am only interested in quality goods. Your friends know that. Nothing but the best." Freddy paused for a sip of coffee. "Last week, someone I trusted sold me a fake diamond. Inexcusable." He nodded toward the thug in the pink suit. "Paco cut off his right index finger. To remind him of his disrespect."

"My friends and I are on the level," I said.

"Just so. I would not have spoken to you otherwise."

"I'll come to the Fenix about the car," I said.

Freddy asked what make of automobile I owned and was pleased to learn it was a utility vehicle. I could not have hoped for better news. Freddy had seen the gangsters. I felt sure of it. He'd talked with Nick. They planned to speak again about the red Pontiac. "*Mañana quizás.*" Freddy had probably bought watches from Shank and Doc. They had to be somewhere in Guad. Freddy thought I was still their friend. That was fine by me. I bid the trio *adiós* and left the Nuevo Léon.

It was 7:20 p.m. The cockfights started in ten minutes. The waiter at the Nuevo Léon told me they ran late. I took the time to drive over to the wrestling matches already under way at the Arena Coliseo Guadalajara. After a search, I parked around the corner on Insurgentes. The Coliseo was painted aqua-blue and glowed like a giant aquarium in the lunar phosphorescence of neon letters spelling out the name beside a sputtering Corona beer sign. Its unadorned bulk reminded me of the old Madison Square Garden on Eighth Avenue where my folks took me to the rodeo and the circus when I was a kid.

Much smaller than either bullring, the Coliseo still seemed plenty large enough. I asked to sit in the most expensive section. The man in ticket box told me the price was the same even though only three matches remained. All the best seats were already sold. I bought a ticket. Past the turnstile, I heard the crowd cheering.

I stepped out of the vestibule into an aisle dividing the two lower sections. A bank of suspended lights glared over the ring like the midday sun. They lit the first six ringside rows. Two plump masked men in colored tights grappled behind the ropes, one green and red, the other all agleam in silver lamé. The white canvas shone bright as a skating rink. I moved along the aisle, ticket in hand, pretending to search for my seat. The place was packed. Few available places remained in the expensive section. I studied the faces sweating under the bright lights. No one looked at me. They cheered as the silver mascara tossed the other one over his shoulder with a dusty thump.

Angling around the Coliseo's vast cube, I searched for familiar faces without success. I felt conspicuous beneath the brilliant lights. Masked wrestling was cheap and dumb enough to attract a *pachuco* crowd. I didn't like the idea of teenage *banditos* on the lookout for me. The section above remained in darkness. I used my binoculars, scanning for someone I recognized. A few women sat scattered throughout the crowd, all Mexican. I circumnavigated the arena in under twenty minutes, not spotting anyone familiar.

Climbing the metal stairs to the balcony where huge windows in the back wall framed the night enclosing the city outside, I had a quick look around. Only a few people perched by the railing, as close as they could get to the action. I gazed down at the gaudy wrestlers clashing like tiny action figures in their square of light. The false heroics magnified my failure.

Back in Bitter Lemon, I found Avenida Revolución on a city map in my Guad guidebook. The cockfighting was all the way out in Tlaquepaque, a twenty-minute drive. I got there after eight thirty. Tired, hapless, bled of all urgency. The Palenque de Gallos was a nondescript place about a mile or so past the Instituto Tecnólogico. I parked on a dark side street wondering what the fuck I was doing. Not having a clue, I asked for a general admission ticket. A mariachi band fiddled inside, charro suits spangling under the lights. I bought four *taquitos* from a woman frying them by the entrance and a can of *cerveza* from a jolly fellow with a washtub full of ice.

A wooden octagon enclosed the small arena called a *palenque*. I found a seat on the steeply tiered pine benches and checked the place out, sipping Tecate. The lights over the ring blazed like those at the coliseum. In the first few rows, the high-rollers' faces gleamed bright as suspects in a lineup. Stragglers sat in the bleachers around me staring at the warbling mariachis. I looked for threatening teenage punks and found only working-class Mexicans. Safe from impending *pachuco* vengence for the moment, I studied the bottom rows through Linda's binoculars until I encountered the feral gaze of a furious gambler glaring back up at me, threat implicit in his dark stare. I lowered the Trinovid.

The music ended and the band filed out of the ring. Two young cockfighters in crisp Levis and cowboy shirts strutted in, lovingly carrying their proud birds to opposite sides of the *palenque*. They stroked the roosters, murmuring to them, kissing their bright coral combs. The fat cats up front studied the cocks, taking a measure of their legs and the aggressive iridescent arc of their tail feathers. The angry gambler turned his back on me. He and his companions laughed and chatted, bottles of booze at their feet.

I'd never been to a cockfight before and watched the seconds come into the ring carrying velvet-lined leather cases. Small stainless-steel scimitars glistened within like jewelry. Each side selected weapons, binding the curved surgical daggers to its rooster's spurs with overlapping lengths of waxed twine. One side used red, the other green. The referee went around, checking things out. He cleansed the blades with a halved lime.

Things got interesting down among the big shots. They shouted their bets at the *corredores*. The bookies waved fingers in the air as the odds changed. Small whispered side bets were transacted in the shadows surrounding me. The crowd grew quiet as the referee drew a line across the dirt in the center of the ring. The two handlers brought their agitated birds to the mark, teasing them back and forth until the ref gave the word.

The roosters rose together into the air, wings thrashing. A dust cloud surrounded their fury like a tiny hurricane. The birds became a tumbling blur. Stray feathers whirled in the air above the conflict. Their fierce cries were lost in the lusty shouting of the crowd. A single silver slash. A sudden bright spurting fountain of blood. The red rooster pierced the neck and breast of the green bird. The wounded cock's handler tried reviving it, blowing a spray of tequila into the gasping bill. His rooster died in his arms. After a *peón* with a straw broom swept up the blood and feathers, a buxom singer accompanied by a guitar player came out to entertain.

Bets paid, the *pez gordo* heavyweights up front drank and relaxed. I didn't need binoculars to make out faces shining clear as bystanders caught in the flash of a Speed Graphic camera. That's when I saw the bald head and gray sharkskin suit in the outer orbit of the power zodiac. Doc! I put the glasses on him to make sure. It was Doc. Gray hair slicked-back along the sides of his gleaming dome, a cigarette caught carelessly in his lips.

Doc looked to have come up in the world over the past couple days. A new suit goes a long way to improve a junky's image. He wore shades and swigged from a bottle of Rémy. The adrenaline jolt focused me like a radar beam. Doc sat alone, drinking and eavesdropping. When the song ended, another pair of roosters made the trip into the ring. Doc tried interesting the guy next to him in a side bet. The Mexican ignored him. Doc waved a handful of bills at a bookmaker.

For the next three fights, I watched only Doc, hearing the raucous cheering without seeing any of the action. I wanted another beer but couldn't risk leaving my seat, afraid he'd slip away when I wasn't looking. Doc drank his way through the bottle of brandy, getting louder as the night wore on. I couldn't hear what he was shouting. The Mexican honchos sitting near him looked annoyed.

Doc bet on every fight. He picked a winner the first two times. Flush with success and booze, he doubled-down on the third contest, waving his cash at a *corredor*. He lost the lot. This led to a shoving match with the bewildered bookie. Two hefty Mexicans rose to the bookmaker's defense. Doc was no longer welcome. Swaying unsteadily in an unsuccessful effort to retain his dignity, Doc grabbed the bottle of Rémy Martin and staggered off like it was his idea.

I jumped from my seat and raced for the exit. A short set of steps led to the empty lobby. I spotted Doc swerving toward the entrance. He didn't see me. I slipped out after him into the dark. He stood at the curb, swilling the last of his cognac. Sneaker-silent, I sprinted toward Bitter Lemon. Why confront a drunk in the middle of nowhere? I wanted Doc to lead me to the others.

A moment of panic when the engine struggled to turn over. Once the van started, I crept toward the corner without turning on the headlights. I stopped where I could see Doc, keeping the motor running. He wove around like a clown about to take a pratfall, looking up and down the avenue. It was well past ten and traffic was light. I considered offering him a ride home.

Headlights approached. Doc tossed the empty bottle against the wall of the Palenque de Gallos and staggered into the street, waving his arms. A cab stopped to pick him up. I waited as they drove off on Revolución before switching on my lights and swinging in behind them. I held back and we rolled along toward Guad. Traffic increased when we entered the city center. The cab moved slower. Other cars provided cover. It felt like a gangster-movie tail job.

The taxi dropped him in front of the Hotel Oriental on Estadio, a cul-de-sac leading to the bus station off the Calzada Independencia Sur. It was a cheap place, a tall narrow building sporting blue-and-green-tiled balconies and wrought-iron lanterns. I parked a little way back on the other side, watching Doc pay the driver and lurch for the entrance. After a moment, I got out, locked the van, and headed after him.

The Hotel Oriental's bleak lobby had the still austerity of a mausoleum. A light glowed in an alcove behind a built-in desk. I rehearsed what I wanted to say and approached the counter. A young man, maybe twenty or so, sat with his nose buried in a textbook. Speaking clearly and slowly in Spanish. I said I had a message for a *viejo* residing in the hotel. I knew him only as Doc, I explained, describing his white-fringed bald head and new gray suit. The night clerk spoke to me in

English. Looking up over his glasses, he said no one fitting my description resided at the Oriental.

"Impossible!" I blurted. "He walked in here two minutes ago."

"That cannot be so." The young clerk kept his face blank as a marble bust. "Our last guest returned more than one hour ago."

"I just saw him."

"You are mistaken, señor."

Nothing more to do. Didn't want to make a scene. Doc must have paid off the staff, a shield against uninvited visitors. *"Gracias,"* I said, heading for the door.

The desk clerk lied about Doc. He'd tip him off about my late-night visit. Probably not until tomorrow. Cheap Mexican hotel rooms don't have phones. I doubted the night-shift scholar would get up off his ass to climb the stairs. Maybe he'd leave a message, maybe not. Doc was no early riser. He'd sleep all morning. Someone new would be at the desk by then.

I thought about camping across the street in Bitter Lemon. What did it matter? Doc was dead to the world at least until noon. To hell with it. I swung the van around, departing Estadio the way I'd come in. The drive back to Rancho Santa Elena took just long enough for me to think things over. Finding Doc in town didn't mean Linda or the others were still hanging around. Didn't prove they'd left, either. Wherever they were, stumbling over Doc was the best piece of luck I'd had in the last three goddamned days.

EASTER
MONDAY

I awoke screaming from a nightmare of fucking Frankie's frozen corpse and got up early, hoping to escape my demons. Things were humming at the trailer park, gringo snowbirds bustling about their motor homes. No way in hell Doc would be stirring at seven thirty in the morning. I brewed a pot of coffee on the Coleman stove and drank a couple mugs before setting off for the cement-block building housing the showers and a laundromat. I carried a sack of dirty clothes and the paperback copy of *Walden* I started reading before my world went mad. While my laundry ran in the coin-operated washing machine, I lost myself in Thoreau's tranquil bean field. When everything tumbled in the dryer, I shaved and luxuriated under my second hot shower in six months.

I took my time back at the van, changing the dressing on my shoulder wound and drinking the last of the java. Around nine thirty, I packed everything away. After paying the manager ten pesos for another night, I drove into town, bought a newspaper, and parked down the block from the Hotel Oriental where I could keep an eye on the entrance. My watch said ten fifteen. I thought of Doc snoring off his hangover inside, and settled down to wait with the local rag, lulled by the growl and grumble of big long-distance buses on their way back and forth from the terminal.

The front page of *El Occidental* had the usual stuff about Guadalajara politics, articles about leftist student protests in Berlin and the widening FBI search for Eric Starvo Galt, suspected assassin of Martin Luther King Jr. At the bottom of the front page, a small box advised expats that today was the final deadline for filing tax returns in the United States.

I found it on page three. A short column under the head *Homicida Junto al Mar*, dateline Barra de Navidad, Jalisco. The body of an unknown foreign woman, possibly North American, had been found several days after death. The Federales described it as a murder although no weapon had been found. That was it. Maybe a hundred words. They didn't know her name. No mention of a cut throat. I read somewhere the police liked leaving certain details of the crime out of their public statements so they could distinguish false nutcase confessions from the real thing.

Around eleven, I got a beer and three tortillas out of the cooler. I sliced an avocado in half with the Randall and spread the creamy fruit onto the tortillas, adding a couple splashes of *salsa picante* for instant tacos. After eating, I took my *antibiótico*. At noon, I popped another *cerveza*. Frankie's prints had to be on file someplace. I wondered how hard the Mexican fuzz would look to find them.

Doc finally limped into the sunlight around one thirty, shaded by a stingy-brim straw hat. He was dressed more casually than the night before, sporting a seersucker jacket over a T-shirt and chinos. He started off down the street. I stepped out of the van, adjusting my belt so the sheathed Randall hung at the base of my spine. The untucked Hawaiian shirt covered it fine. I locked Bitter Lemon and strolled after Doc.

He walked west on Estadio past the Hotel Canadá. A sign painted on the side of the Canadá boasted rooms for fifteen pesos. Doc headed straight for the Terminal de Autobuses at the end of the block. Freestanding six-foot letters on the roof spelled out the name of the seven-story concrete-and-brick building. Even a junky could spot it. I followed him into the bustling bus station lobby. Was Doc getting out of town? He had no luggage. No way he'd leave his new sharkskin suit behind.

Doc wove between passengers waiting with their suitcases and walked into the dining room, heading for the second-class side. I stood in the entrance watching as he found a table and placed his hat carefully on the seat beside him. A trio of waiters looked on. *"Buenos días, Doc,"* I said, straddling a chair opposite the old man.

"Whatdaya say, kid?" He blinked through his green-tinted plastic tortoiseshell shades. "Figured you'd be turning up sooner or later."

"You knew it'd be sooner. The guy at the front desk tipped you off."

"Yeah. Wonderful what fifty pesos a week can buy around here." Doc fumbled a trembling hand inside his jacket. I reached back under my shirt, unsnapping the keeper strap on the Randall. Doc pulled out a crumpled pack of Faros and I relaxed. "How about I buy you lunch?" I said, turning my chair around so it faced the table.

"That's a white man's offer I never say no to." Doc lit a cigarette and shook out the match as the white-jacketed waiter silently appeared. We glanced at our mimeographed gringo-friendly menus. Doc ordered fried eggs, unable to make the waiter understand what he meant about "over easy." I went for the liver with bacon. Together both meals came to a buck fifty. Two beers added another four bits to the tally.

I stared at Doc, watching him smoke and tremble. Maybe he just needed a fix. I began doubting my instincts. Doc's beady eyes darted back-and-forth behind his sunglasses like frantic rats trapped in fish bowls. The man acted nervous as a tomcat at the dog pound. "So, Doc," I whispered, "Where's Linda?"

"How the fuck should I know? Shacked up with Nick someplace."

That one felt like somebody kicked me below the belt. I

didn't want to believe it and swallowed down the lump in my throat, trying hard to show Doc I didn't give a shit. My eyes probably betrayed me.

"Love is strange, kid," Doc said, clocking my expression.

"What's that? More Gibran crap?"

"It's a song, dummy. Don't you ever listen to the radio?

"Fuck the radio! Is Linda okay?" Deep down, I still wanted to believe she was Nick's prisoner.

"Last I saw," Doc grinned slyly at me, "she was happy as a honeymooner."

Another low blow. "Tell me where to find them."

"How the hell should I know. They've got the car, that much I'm sure of."

The stupid gangster-mobile meant nothing to me. "Okay, Doc," I snarled. "Who did it?"

"Did what?"

"Don't be stupid. I'm talking about Frankie."

Doc scratched his cheek. "You don't know who killed her?"

"Did I? Was it me?"

Doc chuckled. "Had a little blackout, eh, kid?" His laughter exploded into hoarse coughing.

"Maybe it was you," I said when his spasm ended, regretting any show of emotion. Doc saw that as a weakness.

"Fuck off!" he said. "You don't know shit. If you was to guess the killer, who'd you pick?"

"Shank," I said.

The waiter arrived at that moment carrying our plates. He set them before us with brisk silent efficiency.

"Pretty sharp for a patsy." Doc sneered at me once the

waiter left. He must have felt in the driver's seat. "Maybe you wouldn't be such a smart-ass if your wife was hanging out with Shank. He'd sure show her some new tricks."

I wanted to reach across the table and punch the old man but held my anger in check. Right now I needed his help. Keeping cool was my best bet. "You're saying Shank killed Frankie?"

"I ain't sayin' nothing of the kind. You take me for a rat? I was maybe suggesting it might have been you killed her. Since you're so ready to lay it off on Shank."

"I didn't kill anybody," I said.

"Killing means nothing to Shank. Less than blowing his nose. Know how he come to get that handle?"

I said I didn't have a clue.

"Just a fish doing his first bit at some nowhere pen in Florida. Probably should of been in high school. Shank gave up on that education shit in eighth grade. Some old chicken plucker spotted him right off. Wants him for his bitch. Beats the crap outta him in the yard under cover of a crowd. Says it'll be worse next time unless they meet up in the showers. Shank makes the date. When he shows, he's got a shiv stashed up his keister. Long thin shank made from a screwdriver he swiped from the furniture shop.

"The plucker tells him to bend over. Shank says, 'Let me make it easy for you,' and soaps up his ass, slipping out the shiv while Big Daddy's getting his hard-on ready. Stuck that jocker so many times he looked like chop suey. Cons called him Shank ever since."

"If the shank fits," I quipped.

Doc ignored me. "The man's dead inside," he growled. "No heart. No soul. No fucking loyalty."

I said nothing, leaning forward to show I was listening. Doc clammed up all of a sudden, poking at his eggs.

"I take it they're all still in Guad?" I said.

"Shank for sure," Doc said. "I keep close tabs on him. Pay a guy at his hotel to call every time he goes in or out."

"How does he do that when you've got no phone?"

"There's one down at the desk." Doc looked at me like I was clueless.

"Maybe Shank's paying that guy to keep him posted about *your* comings and goings."

Doc smiled at the thought. "Shank's a stone killer," he said. "And a crook and a double-crosser. But, one thing he's not. He's not sneaky."

"What about Linda and Nick?"

"They're together someplace with the car. Maybe still here in town. That fuckin' Firebird's half mine. I helped snatch it. Shank, he gave the car over to Nick. Says I'll get my share. Same deal with the watches. Shit! He keeps all the goods and I'm supposed to trust him?

"Show me where he lives," I said.

Doc took off his green shades and stared at me with bloodshot eyes. "'You are not evil when you seek gain for yourself.'" He was quoting Gibran again.

"What's that supposed to mean?"

"Listen, kid, nothing's free in any world I ever lived in. Lemme tell you a little story. Couple guys stick up a jewelry store in Beverly Hills. They get away with a dozen watches. The best. Quality goods. Worth a grand or two each, maybe more. So, they're on the lam and hard up for bread. They sell a couple for three hundred bucks apiece to keep old man wolf from the door. The other guy says he'll take charge of the loot. Sell the watches off one at a time. Get better prices. Can you believe that shit? Tell me he's not about to screw his partner."

I shrugged. "What'd you expect? An unrigged deck?"

"Here's what you got to do for me, kid. You got to back me up when I ask for my fair share. That is to say, if you want a get-together with Shank."

"What do you mean, back you up?"

"You know. Be there for me." Doc made an expansive gesture with his hands. "Who am I kidding? You ain't got the balls for it."

"I'm not afraid of Shank," I lied.

"You fucking well better be. He could kill you with a ballpoint pen." Doc scooped into his egg yolk with a folded tortilla. "Held between his teeth! We go up against Shank, you better come heavy."

"What?"

"Bring a piece."

"A piece of what?" I tried to lighten things up with a joke, but Doc didn't get it.

"A gun, dummy," he grumbled. "A *pistola. Trente ocho.*"

"*Treinta y ocho,*" I corrected.

"Whatever."

"I've got a gun," I said.

"Perfect." Doc grinned. "Maybe we're in business. Got it with you?"

"No."

"How long before you can get it?"

I thought that one over. "Most of the afternoon," I said.

"It'll have to be tomorrow then," Doc said. "This is a daytime thing. I wouldn't want to try and pull it off at night. Shank'd be wise to us if we came after dark."

"I'll be ready tomorrow."

"Meet me here at noon."

"Okay." I got up, placing a banknote *veinte* and a ten-peso cartwheel by my plate. "*Hasta mañana.*"

I left Doc half-thinking the whole deal with Shank might be a con giving the old man time to slip away. Figured I had to trust him. No other choice. I knew it was risky but I needed Doc to get to Shank. Maybe he lied about not knowing Nick's whereabouts. I'd find out tomorrow when we met up with Shank. Lots to do in between.

At a window marked INFORMACIÓN, I said I was a *cazador*, a hunter, and asked for the address of a reputable sporting goods store. The man told me of a place called La Casa del Cazador on the Calle Francisco I. Madero near the corner of Ocho de Julio. The name struck me as too cute to be true. I took a chance and drove over, following Independencia up to Madero and turning left. I had trouble finding a place to park and circled the area until I lucked out and pulled in behind a departing pickup truck a block and a half away from the shop.

La Casa del Cazador turned out to be much smaller than I anticipated. A long painted signboard mounted over the door had the name in faded gilt letters. Displayed behind dusty multipaned show windows flanking the entrance, an odd assortment of duck decoys, poorly mounted pheasants, and various animal skulls suggested a natural history display in a small town museum. A bell tinkled above my head as I entered.

I expected something along the lines of a seedy Mexican pawnshop. Instead, I encountered an elegant old-fashioned establishment with dark wood-paneled walls, beveled mirrors, and a long glass showcase perched on graceful curving legs. It reminded me of the gun room on the seventh floor of Abercrombie & Fitch. A miniature version of the magical place where my dad took me a couple times on those rare occasions when we ventured above 14th Street.

La Casa del Cazador possessed the same atmosphere of polite respectability, inviting gentlemen to come and indulge their love for the trappings and weaponry of blood sport. In place of the stuffed herds of Cape buffalo and kudu overpopulating the gun room, a single mule deer mount hung on the back wall. Abercrombie's platoon of safari-suited salesmen was reduced to a single pewter-haired gentleman wearing a vest and sleeve garters. His blue suit jacket hung over the back of a chair by a desk in the corner. He stood beside a wall rack of shotguns and sporting rifles, regarding me with solemn indifference as I made my way around the shop admiring the arsenal on display.

In place of the splendid Purdey, Boss, and Churchill shotguns for sale at Abercrombie & Fitch, a number of handsome moderately priced Spanish and Italian double-barrels—AYA, Rizzini, Franchi, and Casa J—stood in a gleaming row along the back wall. The proprietor watched me, maintaining a serene detachment until I was only feet away. *"¿En qué puedo servirle?"* His Spanish held a hint of lisping Castillian. He wanted to know how he could be of service.

"Una caja de cartuchos para una escopeta, por favor," I replied, asking for a box of shotgun shells.

"¿Qué caliber de tubo?"

"Doce. Perdigónes doble-cero." I specified twelve-gauge double-ought buckshot.

"Ah, muy fuerte," he observed, placing a box of Aguila cartridges on the countertop.

I didn't care how strong he thought they were and wasn't interested in Mexican ammunition. Grappling for a way of saying this politely, the best I came up with was, *"¿Tiene Federal o Remington? ¿Winchester, quizás?"*

The proprietor frowned, setting a carton of Federals next to the Aguilas. *"Es igual,"* he said, *"pero los otros están mas caro."*

The price didn't matter to me. I was afraid shells manufactured in Mexico might misfire. "Los Federales son buenos," I said. *"¿Cuánto cuesta?"*

He told me the amount, sternly pointing out those of the *Estados Unidos* cost almost twice that of the ammo manufactured by CDM. I said it was okay. With a new tone of arch disapproval, the gun shop proprietor asked what sort of game I planned on hunting.

Caught off-balance, I glanced about evasively. Spotting the mounted buck, I blurted, *"Venado."*

"*¿Como este?*" the man asked. "*No es la temporada.*"

"*Claro,*" I said, knowing full well it wasn't hunting season. "*Me falta practicar.*" I wanted to be more explicit but couldn't remember the word for marksmanship. To change the subject, I paid with one of my silver Olympic coins.

The proprietor picked the twenty-five-peso piece up off the counter. "*Sí,*" he said. "*La puntería es importante.*" He placed extra emphasis in supplying my forgotten word.

I didn't say anything, watching the man wrap the box of twelve-gauge shells in brown paper and string like some drab Christmas present. Not knowing if legal documents were required for shotguns in Mexico, I harbored a nagging fear he was going to ask to see my firearm license. Panic gripped me. I wanted to be out of the shop as fast as possible.

"*Gracias,*" I said, grabbing my package and heading for the door.

"Happy hunting," he called after me in perfect English.

Back in the van, I stared at the small square package sitting on the seat beside me. What the hell difference did it make who made the fucking shotgun shells? I wasn't going to shoot any-body. Why even bother loading the thing? Somehow it made a difference. If I went up against Shank with an empty weapon, he'd know. My eyes would give me away. There are degrees of fear. Shank had a predator's instinct for sensing his opponent's terror. A loaded gun provided insurance against his deadly stare.

I had work to do and needed a quiet spot to get it done. Leafing through my cheap city guide, I came across the perfect destination and drove out of town past the airport on González Gallo. I took Highway 35 eight or nine miles toward Chapala before turning left onto a gravel road, heading for Juanacatlán Falls. The guidebook called it the "largest waterfall in Mexico." I followed signs pointing the way toward *el salto*.

I had no interest in sightseeing and didn't plan on going all the way to the falls. My goal was privacy. I rattled along, checking out the surrounding landscape. After a couple miles, I spotted an isolated grove of trees set well back from the road across an open stretch of rocky scrub. I eased Bitter Lemon over the rough terrain, pulling in among the *madroñas*. Not a house in sight. No livestock grazing nearby. I had the place to myself.

My first task made me nervous. Test-firing the Reilly might prove dangerous. Proper procedure meant securing the shotgun in a vise and pulling the triggers from a safe distance with a length of stout cord. I didn't have a vise. The weapon was useless if it didn't shoot. Better to risk blowing my head off today than guarantee Shank an upper hand tomorrow. I tugged the old side-by-side out from under the sleeping platform.

People do stupid things because they don't foresee the consequences. Ignorance overcame my apprehension. I stuffed a couple shells into the shotgun. What the hell. I thumbed back the side hammers and swung the double barrel to my right shoulder, aiming up over my head. The gun had hair triggers. Kicked like going for a field goal. The stab wound in my left shoulder winced with sympathetic phantom pain at the recoil. The Reilly's breech held tight despite its age. No one around but me to hear the reports, loud as twin thunderclaps.

Ears ringing, I extracted the spent shells. The old smoke pole passed the test even if its bird-hunting days were over. One thing sure, no way in hell Doc and I could get the drop on Shank if we walked in with me carrying a big scattergun. I got out my toolbox and readied a work platform in the van, flipping back the covered foam rubber section cut to fit a hinged plywood storage hatch.

Popping off the Reilly's forearm, I opened the action and removed the barrels from the hinge pin in the receiver. I set the stock aside, snapping the forearm back in place. About two inches above it, I wound a strip of black cloth friction tape around the barrels. Wrapping a towel over the breech, I secured the barrels to the edge of the plywood with a pair of wood clamps.

I took my hacksaw from the toolbox. Using the outer edge of the friction tape as a guide, I cut carefully through both barrels. This proved much easier than anticipated. I smoothed the rough edges around the cut with a mill file and finished the job with a piece of sixty-grade emery cloth. The end result wasn't perfect but good enough for what I had in mind.

I didn't protect the butt end of the stock before clamping it to the plywood. Fitting the hacksaw with a wood blade, I made a cut following the curve of the checkered pistol grip from a point behind the top tang. The old walnut turned out much tougher to saw than steel. I took my time and felt pleased with the results, rounding off the edges with a wood rasp. It looked pretty good, the pistol grip shaped like an old-fashioned handgun. I wrapped the grip with friction tape. Didn't want to drop the sawed-off when my palms dampened with fear.

Shortened barrels back in place, the heavy weapon balanced nicely when I aimed it. Overall, the piece looked about eighteen inches long. No derringer but still easy to conceal. For some reason, I wanted the gun to be clean. I put away my tools and pulled a small rag soaked in white gas through each barrel on a piece of string before going over the Reilly with 3-in-One oil. Bundling the weapon in a towel, I stashed it beneath my sleeping pillow.

I had a war-surplus trenching shovel among my gear. The blade folded over and slipped into a canvas holster. Linda paid two bucks for it at an army navy store south of Market. We used it to dig latrines when camping off road. I tightened the threaded sleeve holding the blade upright and dug a small hole about right for a crapper. Into it, I dropped the severed barrels, the fine walnut stock and two spent shotgun shells. A couple quick shovelfuls refilled the miniature latrine. I tamped the earth down, scuffed the surface with my sneaker, and was on my way.

I torched a fat one on the drive back to Guad, the last dorf in my little tin box. It grew dark when I cruised through the outskirts of town. I had a local Mexican rock-and-roll station playing on the car radio and pulled over to listen to a bluesy new Beatles song, just released a couple weeks ago. I gleaned that and the title, "Lady Madonna," from the frenzied staccato of the dj's machine-gun Spanish. It was a good song, featuring Paul's rollicking Fats Domino–style piano. A tenor-sax jazz solo at the end sent me into dope-fueled memories.

My father had been a jazz fan and turned me on to the

sounds of Art Tatum, Django Reinhardt, Duke Ellington, and Count Basie before I could read. He took me with him to Nick's Steakhouse, the Village Vanguard, Arthur's Tavern, and Café Society, all an easy walk from his own joint on Sheridan Square. I'd sip my Roy Rodgers while he knocked back old-fashioneds, listening to Bud Freeman, Billie Holiday, Roy Eldridge, Earl Hines, and a host of legendary sidemen, all swaying in my mind like a ghostly jiving Greek chorus.

I cherished those childhood moments for the music I came to love and the connection with my dad. The warm rich smell of tobacco on his houndstooth jacket, his easy smile and conspirator's wink. "In the groove yet, kiddo?" he'd say when the music started. Jack Delaney's, my father's restaurant on Grove Street, was a tavern from the twenties decorated with racetrack memorabilia. I figured Jack Delaney had been some famous jockey. All the barstools came with English saddles for seats. I'd rock back and forth, riding a long shot down the homestretch to win by a nose in the photo finish.

Dad bought the place in the middle of the Depression. He hired a cocktail pianist who cranked-out old favorites nightly, a brandy snifter stuffed with greenbacks perched above the keyboard. When I asked him why he didn't get some hot boogie-woogie player to tickle the ivories, Dad said just because he dug jazz, it didn't mean his customers felt the same. Most of the regulars loved the cornball tunes Jack Lane performed on request. Every time I hear someone playing "Melancholy Baby," it brings back memories of my father, wearing a sharp Countess Mara tie, red rosebud in his lapel, smoking and drinking in Jack Delaney's Saddle Bar, where a mounted thoroughbred's head hung high on the wall observing the hilarity with wild glass eyes.

Heading out of town, I stopped for a bite at El Gallo Grill on motel row along López Mateos. They served American-style cooking. I ordered a T-bone steak and mashed potatoes, the perfect last meal for a man on death row. In the end, I wasn't very hungry. I couldn't stop thinking about tomorrow. Trying to keep things positive, I took my penicillin. Seemed like a bet on the future.

After nine, I pulled into my space at the trailer park. Chattering snowbirds sat at picnic tables outside their campers. The blue glow of TV screens lit up the Airstream windows like tropical fish tanks. These aluminum mobile homes all supported antennas, tract houses in a futuristic Martian suburb. I imagined the geezers clustered inside, transfixed by *Bonanza* or *Mannix* or *The Beverly Hillbillies*.

Sitting cross-legged on my bed inside Bitter Lemon with the curtains drawn, I rolled a bunch of dorfs. The Tupperware container labeled OREGANO remained nearly half full. I didn't want to be stoned for my confrontation with Shank. Having something to smoke in celebration afterward introduced a note of false optimism into an unpromising situation. Not ready for sleep, I took a cold beer and a number and went for a walk around the outskirts of my trailer park suburbia.

The small groups were breaking up, retirees shuffling back to their expensive caravans and the dubious comforts of television. None of these squares ever took a stroll in the unfamiliar darkness. The night belonged to me. I'd been a night person since I was a teenager. Jazz was everywhere in Manhattan during the fifties, in bars all over town. Dad had been my ambassador to those dark, smoky establishments when I was a little kid.

A high school sophomore needed no adult supervision. The legal drinking age in New York was eighteen at the time. I started cheating around fifteen. Our passport to nightlife freedom was a fake draft card. A senior at school knocked off blank copies in the print shop and sold them for five bucks each, a hefty sum back when tap beer cost a dime and summer jobs paid a dollar an hour.

My mecca was Birdland, "The Jazz Corner of the World," a basement club on Broadway just north of 52nd Street. Named for Charlie "Yardbird" Parker, who died of heroin addiction at thirty-four the year before I started making the scene, the place pulsed with the urgency of the new. "Through these portals pass the most" was painted on an arch above the ticket window at the bottom of the stairs. Descending toward the smoke and noise seemed a journey into the underworld, the frantic falsetto of the midget emcee screeching like an imp stranded in hell.

I drained the beer foam and took a long last drag on the roach. It burned my fingers and I flicked it away, a tiny meteor arcing into the moonlight. I'd searched for the heart and soul of midnight all my life, a quest as ephemeral as the brief trajectory of the discarded ember. I never found what I was looking for on my nocturnal pilgrimages, always the outsider, yearning to be hip.

Standing in the darkness, watching the trailer lights go off one by one in Rancho Santa Elena, the inevitability of crossing paths with someone like Nick felt preordained. A junky hipster sitting in with jazz greats while doing time. Our eventual meeting began the first night I flashed my fake draft card in some seedy dive where the music played hot and loud. I'd been searching for him all my life.

The Café Bohemia, around the corner from Jack Delaney's on Barrow Street, didn't feature jazz when Dad was alive. I went there at sixteen to hear Miles Davis and his quartet with Red Garland on piano and stood at the bar by the entrance to the long narrow room, nursing a seven-ounce mini-bottle of beer that set me back an unbelievable ninety cents. There was only one band on deck that night. When the set ended, the musicians drifted toward the bar from the bandstand.

As Miles approached, I felt bold enough to stammer, "That was a really beautiful solo you played on . . . 'On Green Dolphin Street,' Mr. Davis."

"How would you know?" the trumpet player growled in his emery-board whisper.

Crawling under the comforter in the van high as the moon, I remembered cringing with adolescent embarrassment. It had been a psychic warning. Watch out for the nightlife, Miles told me. Stop pretending to be something you're not. Beware of drugs and junkies. They'll sell you out every time.

EASTER
TUESDAY

—— • ● • ——

The rising sun woke me from a dreamless sleep. I lay on my back, staring at the van's bare metal roof, unwilling to start the day. It was hours before I was slated to meet Doc at the bus station. No advantage in rushing toward the end of my life. Lounging in bed like I had nothing important to do felt good. The ache in my left shoulder was mostly gone. I taped on a clean bandage. The wound had scabbed over. I lay there thinking about fate. When Bitter Lemon's interior grew hot as an oven, I knew it was time to face the day.

My neighbors on either side bustled about their motor homes. It was a little after eight. Four hours until the show-down. I shaved in the bathhouse and a leisurely *huevos rancheros* breakfast improved my mood. After washing down the penicillin tablet with four cups of black coffee, I daydreamed about Linda. About one time, the first summer we were together, when we went to McSorley's. I started drinking in the old tavern on East Seventh Street at fifteen. They served only ale. Brewed it themselves someplace in Brooklyn. Two mugs for a quarter.

When Linda heard McSorley's was the oldest bar in Manhattan, she wanted to go. When she learned women were not allowed, she insisted on going. We found a threadbare double-breasted suit at a secondhand store, pinning Linda's cinnamon hair up under a sweat-stained Giants cap. A paste-on novelty shop mustache provided the final touch. We brazened our way past a brigade of old Irish codgers standing watch in the front barroom. It felt all electric, not like the many laid-back times I'd been there before. No mouse-in-the-corner shit for Linda. She was the life of the backroom party, making up lies and showing the old drunks how to do the merengue, diagram-ming the fancy footwork on the sawdust-covered floor. I fell in love with her that night, with her wild laugh and flashing absinthe eyes.

I found myself flipping my lucky Olympic coin. What dif-ference did it make if Linda was fucking Nick? A flick of the thumb and the silver disc spiraled into the air. Not if she wasn't hurt. Over and over. She had another boyfriend our first sum-mer. That didn't mean shit in the end. Heads, things would work out okay for me today. Who ever knew for sure? Tails, I'd be dead. Heads . . . ! I flipped the coin again. I wanted her to be alive, no matter what. Heads! Third time lucky? HEADS!

"Call a man's bluff, always pays to hold a good hand," my father once told me. Dad was a gambler and mostly a successful one. I took his advice on the subject as the high roller's gospel. He also said: "A skilled player doesn't need to cheat." He knew the other guy's cards by the look in his eyes. "If you can't keep it deadpan, wear dark glasses."

I pulled the sawed-off Reilly from its hiding place, broke open the action, and slid two fat red shells into the breech. I still didn't plan on shooting anybody but bluffing Shank with an empty gun remained a loser's gambit. A warning round into the ceiling might do the trick. To stop Shank from reading secrets in my eyes, I slipped on a pair of Wayfarer Ray-Bans.

Dad won the money to buy Jack Delaney's during a week-long poker game in Saratoga Springs. He wasn't a horseplayer but said you could always find some action in a crowd of hand-icappers. Owning a restaurant with a racetrack theme was a coincidence. The place attracted a sporting crowd looking for the sort of action my father provided in the game he ran in the Hay Loft, an unused upstairs dining room.

"Best thing is playing on your home turf," Dad said. "Gamble in unfamiliar territory; don't get caught with an ace up your sleeve. You'll beat the long odds only if you play it straight." His words sang in my memory as I put the sawed-off shotgun at the bottom of the straw *bolsa* and covered it with a towel. My ace in the hole. Driving out, I stopped at the office and paid for one more night in advance. Another bet on the future. Things might come up heads after all.

I parked in front of the bus station by eleven fifteen. After buying the morning papers at a newsstand in the main lobby, I found a quiet table off to the side of the second-class restaurant and ordered a large chocolate atole. Leafing through the newspapers, I searched for further news about Frankie. It seemed impossible. Not a single mention of Barra de Navidad or anyone murdered there.

Maybe it made sense after all. The Federales didn't know Frankie's identity if the gangsters did their job right when they stripped the place. The Díaz family wouldn't be much help. We all paid rent in cash. Never provided any personal identification. Maybe they could describe our cars. Thousands of VW buses and red muscle cars must rumble around Mexico.

The fuzz didn't have much more than a dead Caucasian female of uncertain nationality found naked with her throat cut. Only Frankie's fingerprints and her distinctive tattoos. Good bet the Federales would make her for an American hooker. Frankie was bound to have a record. Her prints were on file someplace. They'd ID her sooner or later. This would lead to Nick, maybe the others. It would take time. Lots of time. Time just might be on my side.

"What's that shit you're drinking?" Doc's rasping voice interrupted my musing. "Looks like cat puke."

I noticed his watery eyes and gin blossom nose. The cheap plastic sunglasses were tucked in a shirt pocket. "Well, well, well," I said. "My man, Doc. This must be tomorrow."

"'For their souls dwell in the house of tomorrow, which you cannot visit, not even in your dreams.'"

"Cut the prophetic Gibran bullshit."

Doc took the chair opposite me. "You should pay some attention, kid," he said. "A little prophecy might be just what the doctor ordered."

"If that's what I needed, I wouldn't be sitting here with you."

"Maybe so." Doc's hand trembled as he reached for the menu. He hadn't shaved, and the silver stubble on his chin added to his down-and-out appearance. "I need some breakfast. You gotta help me with the lingo."

The white-jacketed waiter appeared at our table, silent as mist. Doc's nervous bloodshot eyes darted up, a con glancing sideways at the screws. He made an attempt at ordering. It came out sounding like "hooves and jawbone." He looked at me in desperation. "Get me some ham and eggs, will ya please, kid."

I straightened things out with the waiter, telling him my "uncle" wanted his eggs *frito* with *pan tostado* instead of tortillas. Doc salvaged enough Spanish to ask for a *café con leche*. The waiter pretended to understand him, gliding off with a polite nod.

"You bring some heat?" Doc whispered.

"It's in the car."

"Good job, kid. Keep it handy when we pay Shank our little visit. Remember, I do all the talking."

I took a long sip of atole, staring at Doc's shifting eyes. "So . . . What is it you want to talk to him about?"

"Weren't you listening yesterday?" he sneered. "The man owes me for some watches."

"I don't give a shit about your fucking watches!"

Doc looked hurt. "Ain't like I won't cut you in for a share."

"Fuck the goddamn share." The waiter approached with Doc's breakfast.

We sat in silence until he left, carrying away my empty bowl and plate. "Don't know I'd trust anybody who didn't want a piece of the action," Doc said, eyes on the departing waiter.

"I want something, Doc," I said. "I'm not in this for kicks."

"Spill it."

"I want my wife."

"No problem. She's with Nick. Sure as shit, Shank knows where they're at."

"I need to know who killed Frankie."

Doc toyed with his eggs. "The prey invites the predator," he mumbled.

"What's that supposed to mean?"

"Philosophy, kid."

I'd had enough fucking philosophy. Doc finished his breakfast. "Where's Shank holing up?" I asked as he shoved the last corner of toast into his mouth.

"Hotel Roma, over on Juárez. Son-of-a-bitch is paying fifteen bucks a night, and me, I'm stuck in a two-bit shit hole. He's even got a fucking swimming pool up on the roof."

"Shank's in fat city. Hot watches must be boss business."

"What am I telling you? He's screwing me. You 'n' me are paying a little visit on old pal Shank to collect what's owed."

"That's got nothing to do with me," I said. "I don't give a shit if you never see a fucking dime out of this. I'm coming along to get what I want."

119

"You said you'd back me up."

"So I did. Safety in numbers. Not interested in helping you shake Shank down."

"This is no shakedown. He owes me the dough, fair and square."

"That's your problem, Doc. Get it any way you can. I'm not strong-arming Shank."

"Just watch my back when we get there is all I'm asking."

"Which will be never if we sit around rapping all day."

"Rapping? That what we're doing?"

"Yeah. You know, shooting the shit."

"No kidding?" Doc's hollow chuckle escalated into a rasping cough. "For me, a rap was always the bit for some crime. Like maybe you got a bum rap. Or if you was lucky, you might beat the rap."

"The beauty of language, Doc," I said, waving for the waiter.

When he approached, Doc said, "Listen, kid, I'm still a little short."

"Guess I'll take the rap for this," I joked, asking for *la cuenta*.

"I'll make it up to you. Buy us a big steak dinner. All the trimmings. After I collect from Shank."

"Why am I not holding my breath?" I paid the bill, which didn't come to much.

"Whadya care who killed Frankie?" Doc asked as we walked across the terminal waiting room.

"I want to know if it was me or not."

"Who can see deep into the unknown," he muttered. "What do we know of truth? Unsolvable riddle or universal law? Ask the immortals for the answer." I had no idea if Doc was quoting Gibran again or just making this shit up as he went along. He went on and on. More dumb crap about truth and justice and the universal mind. He wore his shades so I couldn't tell if he was putting me on. I let him keep it up all the way to the parking area.

I unlocked Bitter Lemon. Doc slid in on the passenger side. "Lemme see your piece," he barked as I settled behind the wheel. I reached over and pulled my *bolsa* up front, flipping back the towel to show him the sawed-off. Doc whistled in appreciation. "Heavy artillery," he said. "That should grab Shank's attention right away."

I drove down Estadio and took a right on Independencia, flowing north with the traffic. Nagging whispers of dread filtered through my mind, shudders of fear trembling in my guts.

"Never seek to understand the labyrinth of the human heart," Doc whispered. "Are we all not lost? Strangers wandering through a dark wood? Stay, pilgrim. Hear my tale. I am but a wanderer in the wilderness. Another who travels into oblivion." I wondered if this was the philosophy according to Doc or some kind of whacko Gibranesque litany. More random snatches from *The Prophet*. I didn't give a shit and tried not to listen.

After maybe fifteen blocks, I turned left onto Juárez. The Hotel Roma sat four blocks further west on the corner of Degollado. I was lucky to find a parking spot close by. My *bolsa* weighed a hundred pounds when I lifted it from the van. After locking Bitter Lemon, I fished in my pocket for loose change, and bought two hours, dropping eight dos décimos coins into the meter.

"Remember, kid, let me do the talking," Doc muttered. We sauntered toward the hotel under flowering jacaranda trees.

"Try not to piss him off."

"Shank was born pissed-off," Doc said.

Not quite a first-class hotel, the Roma was a palace compared to the dump where Doc hung his hat. Faux-antique furniture clustered upon kaleidoscopic Persian carpets demarcating the lobby like vivid islands on a gray terrazzo sea. A guy with a mop worked hard keeping the floor agleam. We were easy to spot—two seedy gringos in sunglasses—yet no one at the front desk watched us make our way toward the elevators.

The lift door shut, final as the fall of a guillotine's blade. An all-pervasive dread numbed my senses. A condemned man, I stared at the slowly ascending floor numbers lighting up one after the other. Doc fidgeted beside me. "When we get to Shank's room, keep your cannon out of sight," he said. "I don't mean cover it with a towel like you're the fucking waiter. Hold it down alongside your leg where he can't see it. Don't show him no heat until we're inside."

"Okay." I tried sounding upbeat without much success.

The elevator stopped when the number five turned red. "All men cross the portal to an unknown future," Doc said as the door slid open.

"Spare me any more Gibran shit."

"Give me some credit, kid. That one was mine."

Doc led me down the carpeted hall, holding his finger to

his lips like Abbott guiding Costello into a haunted house. Outside room 504, Doc used his hands in a pantomime, deaf-mute sign language all his own. He signaled me to put the *bolsa* off to the side against the wall. I pulled out the sawed-off, cocking the hammers and holding it behind my legs. The whole absurd Keystone Kops aspect heightened my terror.

Doc tapped on the door. No reply inside. "Don't want to knock too loud," Doc whispered, "or you'll sound like the law." He knuckle-rapped shave-and-a-haircut again with more gusto.

After a moment, Shank snarled, "Who is it?"

"It's me. Doc."

"Go away."

I looked at Doc and shrugged. What now? Doc knocked again. "Let me in."

"Get the fuck away from here!"

I felt a surge of relief. The whole deal was over before it started. I knew where Shank lived. I could wait for him on my own, ferret-out Nick and Linda's location in a more congenial way.

"Come on, Shank," Doc pleaded. "Don't be such a hard-ass. This is important."

"Not interested."

"I brought a little taste."

Another long pause. "Whatcha got?" Shank's voice was right behind the door.

"It's a surprise," Doc said. "Open up."

One more pause. Then, the knob-lock clicked. "Better be good," Shank rasped, opening the door. He was barefoot, dressed all in black as usual. His slitted eyes looked dead.

He stared at me without interest. "This your big surprise?" he asked.

"The kid brought some killer kabayo." Doc patted me on the shoulder. "He's a good kid."

Shank's lifeless eyes burned into me. I felt my Wayfarers melting. "Riding the train now, Toddy-boy?" His voice showed no trace of interest or emotion. "Well, let's cook it up. Come on in. I'll punch your ticket."

We stepped into Shank's room. Doc closed the door behind him, pulling the security chain along in its slot. Shank had definitely come up in the world. The place boasted wall-to-wall carpet with matching drawn drapes. No sunlight penetrated his murky abode. The only true illumination came from a lamp on the bedside table. A tray of leftover room service breakfast sat on the desktop. A scattering of black clothes littered the floor. The unmade bed faced a soundless TV glowing in a mahogany cabinet. Shank leaned against the bathroom doorframe. "So," he said with his death's head grin, "let's see some of this surprise horse you rode in on."

"Show him, kid," Doc said, raising his right arm like a make-believe gunslinger.

This is it, I thought, swinging the Reilly into sight. I gripped the forearm with my left hand.

Shank never flinched or blinked. He stared hard at us without any change of expression. "Guess you must think you got the bulge on me, Doc," he said. "What with the kid here packing."

"We need to talk, Shank," Doc said.

"About what? How you plan on trimming me?"

"It's not like that. This ain't no shakedown."

"No? Whatd'ya call it then?"

Doc fidgeted. "Kind of a fact-finding mission." He tried sounding conciliatory.

Shank still hadn't moved, leaning casually in the bathroom doorway as if we were nothing more than hotel maids delivering fresh towels. "No problem, then. Ask away. I'll give it to you straight."

Doc jerked his head at me. "The kid's got a question first."

"Shoot." Shank's cold Jolly Roger smile widened. "Just an expression."

"Where can I find Nick and Linda?" I held the sawed-off steady despite my shaking hands.

"Young Tod, the jealous husband. Gonna blow the lovebirds down?"

His words bit like an icy wind. "N-nothing like that," I stammered. "I could never hurt Linda. Just need to talk, is all."

"Take me for a sap," Shank said. "I think you're on the square. They're holed-up in Guanajuato. Don't think they're doing much talking."

Doc cleared his throat. "One more thing," I said. They both looked at me, annoyed.

"Why not," Shank sneered, "if it's jake with your high pillow here?"

Doc shook his head negatively, a signal of displeasure Didn't matter. I was risking my neck for him and had to get it out. "Did you kill Frankie?" I asked Shank, meeting his unblinking gaze.

"Who told you that?"

Not meaning to I glanced sideways at Doc. "Nobody," I lied. Too late.

"Well, you heard wrong." Shank glared hard at Doc. "The shindig had gone bughouse. We was all jingle-brained. I needed some air. Took a long walk on the beach. Most of the way to Hotel Melaque. When I got back . . ." He looked straight at me. "You was sacked out with a stiff. What about you, Doc? Where was your ass when Frankie croaked?"

"Funny you put it that way." Doc sounded steady and clear. "As it happened, I had the runs that night. You know me and the old Montezuma's revenge. I was in the crapper when Frankie got cut. Stepped out and you was in the room. Back from your walk. Lover boy was bare-assed next to Frankie. All covered in blood. I figured the both of 'em got rubbed out."

A long silence followed Doc's self-serving recital. For all I knew, they were a pair of liars. I should have played it smart and left right then. I had all I needed. What did I owe Doc? Not a damn thing. Like a sucker, I stuck around.

"Okay, Doc," Shank said at last, "you didn't just fall by so the kid could give me the third degree. Spill it!"

Doc found it necessary to stare at his shoes. "You owe me," he mumbled.

"Owe you fucking what?"

"Plenty. Can't say how much for sure. Them watches was half mine. I was in on the heist."

Shank laughed. It sounded like the cough of a leopard. I knew he meant it for a laugh. "You couldn't steal day-old doughnuts from a soup kitchen."

"That's not fair, Shank," Doc pleaded. "I was in on the caper. And that Pontiac. It was me spotted the Firebird."

Shank shook his head in a parody of disbelief. "What were you gonna do? Push it all the way to Mexico? I hot-wired the fuckin' thing."

All the energy seemed to go out of Doc. He sagged like a snowman in the early spring sun. "I was there," he whined. "Took the same risk. I should get my share."

"Tell you what." Shank held out his open palms to show he was a right guy. "Nick's got the car. When we get around to selling it, we'll cut you in for a third."

"I should get half. Why does Nick get a share?"

"Nick is our connection to Freddy," Shank explained patiently. "Without Freddy, we got zip. This way, we collect several large. Concerning them watches, there was twelve in all. I sold four. Considering it was my heist, I figured it for a fair dib. There's eight left. To show I'm on the square, I'll split the sugar with you. You get four today. How's that sound? Sell 'em on your own."

"Sounds darb," Doc said. "Who gets to pick?"

"I ain't no fence? You, neither." Shank gestured toward a bedside table. "What do we know about watches? All top-notch goods. Got 'em in the satchel over there. Whatd'ya say I reach in. Grab four without looking. Like the lottery?"

Doc thought the proposition over. "Deal," he said. "Drink out of the same bottle."

Shank walked across the room. I kept the sawed-off trained on him. He snapped open his satchel and reached inside, all the while looking right at Doc as he groped in the bag, feeling around for a handful of watches. "Wish I'd thought of this up front," he said. "It's all silk now."

"Always knew you to be aces," Doc said.

Shank's hand came out of the leather satchel. "Fuck you, Doc!" he shouted, shooting the old man smack in the middle of his chest with a snub-nosed revolver. In the same instant, I flinched and the shotgun discharged. The full charge caught Shank in the side and sent him crashing back against the wall like a man tossed by a bull. He slid splay-legged to the floor. A smear of gore marked his path down the floral wallpaper.

I stared in horror, ears ringing from the Reilly's thunderous report, not comprehending what had just happened. The air stung with an acrid smell of cordite. Shank sat staring at me, his back against the wall. The load of buckshot had torn his black T-shirt into a bloody purple pulp. His right arm dangled from the shoulder socket like a broken doll. I fought to keep from puking. Shank reached across his body with his left hand, groping for the pistol still gripped uselessly in his right. "Should of . . . done you . . . first," he gasped.

I watched his fingers feeling blindly for the gun, terrified I'd have to shoot him again. Shank's eyes burned, not in hatred but with grim determination. He glared up at me and seemed to lose focus, his fierce stare glazing over like congealing fat. His head sagged, drooping down onto his ruined chest.

I looked over at Doc. He lay flat on his back, arms at his sides. A large red stain bloomed in the center of his white guayabera shirt. Bubbling blood-froth gurgled from his nose and mouth. Why didn't he see it coming? Doc knew Shank hid knives up his ass. Me? I was the patsy fall guy. What did I know?

"Doc . . . ?" I implored.

He didn't answer. His eyes stared sightlessly at the ceiling as the almost imperceptible rise and fall of his breathing ceased altogether. The silence felt tangible.

Someone might come at any moment, the shots loud enough to be heard down in the lobby. My mind raced. I stared at the sawed-off shotgun in my hand wanting to be rid of it and hurried into the bathroom. Gagging back nausea, I grabbed a hand towel off the rack and carefully wiped down the Reilly. Back in the bedroom, I knelt and pressed the weapon into Doc's open right hand, curling his pudgy fingers around the grip. My gorge rose again at the touch of his clammy flesh. This much blood made me sick. I needed things to look right, taking the time to guide Doc's forefinger onto the front trigger.

My heart rioted as I struggled to compose myself, trying to get my story straight in case somebody found me in the room. At the door, I used the hand towel to draw back the chain and turn the knob. I eased it open a crack and peered into the hall. The coast looked clear in both directions, corridor quiet and deserted. It seemed impossible. No one was there. Nobody rushing to investigate the commotion.

I leaned against the door, thinking things over in a panic. Had I left it all just right? I never touched anything in the room but the shotgun. That was clean of my prints. Best to split right away. A last-second afterthought had me grab Shank's leather satchel. I snapped it shut and used the hand towel to let myself out.

Picking up my *bolsa*, I dropped in the towel and bypassed the elevator, making for the fire stairs. Didn't want to meet a hotel detective on his way up. I took the stairs at a normal pace trying not to make any noise or seem like a man in a hurry. Five flights later, I emerged at the far end of the lobby. The guy with the mop still swabbed away. He didn't notice me.

The front desk stood out of my line of sight. I left the Hotel Roma by a side entrance on Degollado, strolling casually around the corner onto Juárez, my bolsa in one hand, Shank's satchel in the other. I resisted an urge to glance into the hotel lobby as I walked past the entrance. The terror fueling my racing heart urged me to run. I forced an appearance of composure, sauntering along like a window shopper.

There was an hour and a half left on the meter when I reached Bitter Lemon. It seemed impossible. Only thirty minutes had gone by. I unlocked the passenger door, tossing in the satchel and *bolsa*, leaning across the seat to pull the lock button on the driver's side. Hair triggers saved my life. Moments later, I cruised along Juárez, heading west with the traffic. I made sure not to speed or try anything tricky. Kamikaze Mexican drivers cut me off at every opportunity. Glancing in the rearview mirror, I anticipated flashing red lights. Patrol cars in rapid pursuit. After Juárez passed through the Parque de la Revolución, I became just another bit of motorized flotsam moving along with the flow.

Past the University of Guadalajara, Juárez transformed into Vallarta. The number of cars thinned out. I felt more conspicuous, and held to the exact speed limit. With every passing block, Hotel Roma and the ghastly occupants of room 504 receded further and further behind me. I passed under Los Arcos, a huge double arch spanning both lanes of traffic. It celebrated an event no one remembered. Just one more extravagant monument in a nation addicted to grandiose civic displays.

I swung out around the Glorieta de la Minerva, where a tall statue of the armored Roman goddess stood encircled by jetting fountains. Rounding the circle, I saw a guy standing under the tamarind tree next to a large green metal box. A handmade cardboard sign advertising HIELO leaned against the tree trunk. I pulled over needing something normal in my life and bought a five-kilo chunk of ice. The *vendedor* helped me pour the meltwater out of my cooler. Badly wanting a drink, I found the Herradura and a pair of amber *caballitos* made from melted beer bottles. I bought them in Colima during my shopping spree for downers, paying triple the glass factory price. The iceman's gold-studded smile widened when I offered him a slug. I uncovered my salt and a lime, which he cut up on top of his green chest.

I filled the two tall shot glasses close to the rim. We said, "*Salud,*" knocking them back in single swallows. The fiery fluid flowed through my system like a tonic.

"¿*Otro más?*" I asked.

His brilliant grin announced I was his true amigo now. We did another and the warm glow in my gut burned away the sick feeling left over from so much blood. I snapped the cap off a bottle of Pacífico, offering one to the *vendedor*. He shyly said he'd prefer more tequila, so I poured him a third shot.

Sipping beer, I leaned into the van and took the Guadalajara guidebook from the glove compartment. I leafed through it, coming across an old photo of Los Arcos taken shortly after it was built in 1942. It stood in the middle of nowhere back before the city expanded, looking as lonely as I felt inside. With no help from the city guide, I unfolded the Gulf Oil road map across the front seat to figure out the best way to Guanajuato. Shank's leather satchel sat unopened on the floor like an admonition. All the tequila in Mexico would never erase the memory of his gory chest and dismembered arm, life fading from his eyes like clouds covering the sun.

I saw from the map that I was on the wrong side of town. Not a happy discovery. Getting out of Guad on the double seemed the way to go. Highway 80 to 110 was the shortest route to Guanajuato, but the road map didn't show access connections in any detail. I went back to the city guide and studied its foldout street plan. Far as I could tell, I needed to go through Tlaquepaque and then Tonalà.

I collected the tequila bottle and my *caballitos*. The iceman asked where I was from. I thought of saying New York. He'd seen my California plates so I made it San Francisco. Why arouse any suspicions?

"*¿Adónde va?*" he asked as I loaded the cooler and the rest of it into my VW.

"Querétaro," I told him, not about to give up my actual destination. I still harbored an insane suspicion the law might be hot on my trail. Better cautious and paranoid than careless and behind bars. We shook hands and he wished me a safe journey. *"Buena suerte,"* I said, off on the road again.

I didn't want to go back past the Hotel Roma so I took the long way around to the center of town following López Mateos, a broad boulevard renamed last year for the ailing former president lingering in his coma, a personification of the country he ruled with an iron fist such a short time ago. I turned left on Niños Heroes, longing to be out of Guadalajara. They say dead men tell no tales. I didn't know what Shank or Doc carried in their pockets. What they might have scribbled down in their rooms. Some stray scrap of paper with my name on it.

In spite of the madhouse macho traffic, I kept the microbus chugging ahead at the speed limit. California plates were a fuzz magnet. The safest road to freedom ran straight and narrow. Once I turned onto Revolución, I breathed a little easier. The cheap tourist pottery shops of Tlaquepaque lay straight ahead. I longed for a smoke and another beer. Logic insisted nobody was after me. A nagging dread kept my eyes darting to the rearview mirror.

I rattled over the cobblestone streets of Tlaquepaque. Revolución somehow became Route 80. Apprehension and terror rode beside me. Strange not feeling any guilt. I suffered greater remorse the time I shot a cottontail, bird hunting with Dad. I held the limp soft creature up by one leg and wept. Shank's torn, bloody body provided a ghastly shock, one I knew would haunt my dreams for the rest of my life, but I shed no tears for the diminutive killer. Shank was vermin through and through. Seeing him slumped mangled against the wall meant no more to me than looking at a squashed cockroach. Only Buddhists mourn dead bugs.

Doc had asked me to bring a piece along, but I didn't do it for him. I wanted to find Linda. His death was just another statistic in tomorrow's news. Doc knew what he was up against and decided to buck the odds. Probably picked the wrong sidekick. That wasn't my fault. I risked my neck for the old man, which evened the score, final tally be damned. Doc rolled the dice. They came up snake eyes. He crapped out.

After passing numerous adobe brick kilns about ten miles further on 80, I crested a hill and descended to a long narrow bridge at the entrance to Zapotlanejo, a small pueblo with a central plaza and adjoining municipal market. Keeping an eye out for kids playing on the road, I eased through town, drunk enough to run someone over if I wasn't careful. After consulting the map, I took a left turn to Lagos de Moreno and straight onto Highway 110. Soon it was all open country. Scattered cornfields and pastureland divided by irregular rock walls. Modest adobe homes dotted the landscape.

Near the top of a hill, a desolate dirt tract carved away from the paved road. I turned off and bounced along until the highway was no longer in sight, easing across open country, coming to a stop in the dead center of nowhere. I dug a brew out of the cooler and fired-up a dorf, sagging like a deflating balloon against the left front tire. Sitting there, blank as a stump, drifting off into oblivion, I left the bloodbath behind like a forgotten nightmare.

After a second joint, more *cerveza*, and a couple swigs of

tequila, the day's horrors floated away on a cloud of intoxication. I struggled to my feet, stoned, ready at last to confront the sordid remnants of disaster. Shank's leather satchel sat on the passenger-side floor, pregnant with menace. I stared at the bag for a while before lifting it onto the seat and unsnapping the clasp.

A squat black semiautomatic pistol, lethal as a sleeping tarantula, lurked inside. After a moment's hesitation, I reached for the weapon. It felt heavier than it looked, a pound and a half or better. The pistol fitted snug in my hand. I had never touched an automatic before but saw at a glance the safety was off. Why did Shank choose the little snub nose over this more effective instrument of death?

The compact pistol, not much bigger than the palm of my hand, had seen some use. The right side of the slide was marked "P. BERETTA-CAL. .9. CORTO-MO 1934-BREVET." Below that, "GARDONE. V.T. 1941 XIX." Almost as old as me. Probably a war trophy brought home from Italy. A quarter century does not make a sidearm an antique. The Reilly was three times older and still got the job done.

I gingerly set the Beretta down on the floor, barrel pointed away. Never pays to be stupid, especially when stoned. Examining the bag revealed four wristwatches, a roll of banknotes, two boxes of ammunition, a worn billfold, an unused syringe in a cellophane package, Shank's linoleum cutter, three bottles of four-milligram instant-release Dilaudid tablets, and at the very bottom, a travel brochure.

I looked at the watches first: a Patek Phillipe with a lizard band, a pair of Rolexes—one a lady's 18-karat white-gold model with a diamond-encircled dial, the other, a hefty Oyster Perpetual in platinum—and last, a classy French number, a Breguet, perhaps the best of the lot. Shank lied to Doc. He claimed to have eight watches. Guess he figured more would better bait his trap.

Such beautiful watches. I'd never seen anything like them in my life. My father wore a slim gold Bulova, but it ranked with Mickey Mouse timepieces next to these beauties. I had no idea what they were worth. A small fortune, I guessed. They seemed to embody the essence of success and prestige. Beverly Hills prices probably way higher than selling to a Guadalajara fence but they'd still bring plenty dinero.

I pulled the rubber band off the fat roll of Mexican currency. All in one-hundred and five-hundred peso notes. I counted the *quinientos* first. Sixty-five. I counted again to make sure. The tally of hundreds came to eighty-three. Altogether, the bundle held 40,800 pesos. I had to use a pencil stub and the margin of my roadmap for calculations. The grand total in greenbacks was $3,264.00. More jotting and mental math led me to conclude that Shank had sold eight of the stolen watches for between five and six hundred dollars. With the proceeds, he'd bought a pair of handguns and enough Dilaudid to keep him high for a month in his comfortable hotel room. The big wad was what was left over.

Snuffing Shank turned out to be a profitable move even if it was an accident. I had more than three grand in cash, watches worth at least another two, plus the Beretta and the drugs. Not much for a life but good value for scum like Shank. I picked up his billfold. Touching it disgusted me. I found a Visa card from the Beverly Hills caper belonging to Nathan R. Schwartzman, another 870 pesos in cash, and a couple slips of Hotel Roma notepaper scrawled with phone numbers. Other documents included an Oklahoma driver's license, a Social Security card, and a membership in the NRA, all signed Burton Breitenbach. A connection to the square's life Shank had long abandoned.

I added the cash to the bankroll and tossed Shank's wallet aside along with his wood-handled linoleum knife. On second thought, I fished the lists of phone numbers out of the discarded billfold, thinking they might prove useful in the future. Next, a look at the travel flyer, wondering where Shank wanted to go. Another clip for the Beretta lay beneath it.

The trifold brochure advertised Guanajuato, a color photo of the extravagant Teatro Juárez adorning the cover. The Doric columns and crown of bronze statues above the portico made it look like a European import. I unfolded the tripart flyer. Small black-and-white pictures illustrated important local attractions on the side panels, flanking a squiggle-line map of the city. Places of interest, hotels of the better class and restaurants offering more than tacos were enumerated along its length.

Close to the bottom stood the Jardín de la Unión. Across from it, Teatro Juárez ranked number three. On the opposite side of the tiny plaza, Shank had drawn an X beside number four, which the map legend identified as the Posada Santa Fé. By the hotel's name, he had added "4/18." Nick was surely staying at the posada. Why would Shank tell me his friend was in Guanajuato if he planned on joining him two days later?

A chilling possibility haunted my stoned thoughts. Shank told the truth because he planned to kill me. "Should've done you first," his last words. Why didn't he? I pointed a gun at him. Shank figured I'd never have the guts to pull the trigger. He plugged Doc instead. The Reilly had hair triggers. End of story.

Jumpy nerves saved my life. I picked the Beretta up off the floor and held it flat on my palm, studying the weapon. Compact and ugly from the snub pout of its protruding barrel to the curious knurled hammer. Metal-rimmed Bakelite grips adorned with an ornate embossed PB monogram near the butt. A lanyard half-loop arced out of the right-hand frame. Efficient and well designed.

What little I knew about semiautomatic pistols came as a teenager watching old gangster movies in 42nd Street triple-feature rerun houses. The hammer was down. I knew why Shank had gone for his revolver. The Beretta was single-action and had to be cocked before it would fire. This meant pulling back the slide. Took a couple extra seconds. Shank wanted the element of surprise.

Gripping the Beretta felt like slipping on a glove. A forward-curving extension of the magazine curled around my pinkie, while an opposing protrusion cast into the frame embraced the back of my thumb. "All guns are loaded," my father taught me. Aiming the compact automatic at the ground, I wanted to test my single-action theory. I squeezed the trigger. Nothing happened. No pull. I guessed right. Dad also said only to aim a weapon at something you planned on shooting. Maybe killing Shank wasn't an accident after all.

I thumbed the magazine release button on the butt of the Beretta, popping the clip. Pulling back the slide, I saw no cartridge in the chamber. I fished the two boxes of ammo out of the satchel. One contained .38 Special rounds; the other was marked .380 APC. I had no idea which one fit the automatic, so I pried a bullet out of the magazine. It matched the .380, the smaller of the two shells. Another reason Shank picked his snub-nosed revolver. The .38 Special packed more firepower.

The Beretta was marked ".9 CORTO" on the right of the slide. I figured this to be .9 millimeter short. *Corto* meant "short" in Spanish, probably in Italian, too. The little automatic was chambered for .9 millimeter short, obviously the same caliber as .380 APC. Figuring all this out felt very satisfying in a smug-stoned way.

I had to learn how to use the Beretta. If Nick was holding Linda prisoner, he'd never let her go without a fight. I assumed he was carrying. Next time I pointed my gun at someone I wanted to shoot, I'd better be damn sure I could hit him. I fished a couple empty smoked oyster tins from my cardboard trash box and placed them on the ground a dozen paces from the VW, propped upright with small stones.

Pushing a clip into the Beretta, I gripped the pistol in my right hand, my finger off the trigger and took hold of the serrations on the rear of the slide, pulling it firmly back, racking a bullet into the chamber. I released the slide and it snapped into place leaving the hammer fully cocked. Wary of clumsy stoned accidents, I turned the safety back to cover the small red dot by the grip.

I took a stance about fifteen feet in front of the two tin cans. Rotating the safety off the red dot until it covered an impressed letter S, I slipped my forefinger inside the trigger-guard and, lining up my target, squeezed off a shot. A sharp report, not nearly as loud as I expected, accompanied a spray of dirt about a foot from the nearest can.

The Beretta had a crisp trigger pull and not much recoil. I took my time with my next shot, gripping my gun hand from underneath with my left to steady it. This one hit the can and it bounced a couple feet away. I managed to score with two out of the remaining five shots. After popping the empty clip, I inserted the spare and pulled back the slide with greater assurance.

Six hits out of seven shots this time. The cans were about the size of a man's forehead. Fifteen feet seemed a reasonable distance. I'd been only half that far from Shank. The box of .380 ammo contained fifty cartridges. I'd just used thirteen. After reloading the two magazines, the carton was half-empty. Maybe I needed more practice but I seemed to have the hang of it. For some nutty reason, it was important not to waste the bullets.

Before hitting the road, I cleaned things up. I put five hundred pesos from Shank's bankroll in my wallet and hid the rest in the secret compartment behind the dash. The Beretta and the box of .380 APC cartridges went back into the leather satchel. I had no use for the .38 Specials or my twelve-gauge shells. They were a liability. Wouldn't be good if the Federales ever pulled me over and found them. Having the same ammunition used in a deadly Hotel Roma shootout was bad news.

I walked a couple hundred yards from the microbus with my war-surplus trenching shovel to a spot where I could no longer see my tire tracks and dug a bucket-size hole. Gathering up the bullet-punctured cans and incriminating ammo along with Shank's wallet, syringe, and linoleum cutter, I dropped in each item one at a time before refilling my tiny grave. Even after smoothing over a last shovel-load of topsoil, the surface looked disturbed. A good hard rain might do the trick. Not likely in the dry season.

Sunlight glinted on a spent shell casing. I scurried around, picking them up, and collected nine out of the thirteen I'd fired. After popping a beer with my church key, I torched a dorf and bounced slowly back to the paved road in first gear. Ice-cold swallows lubricated my dry throat. Inhaling a final toke, I flipped the roach out the window. We'd save them all back in Frisco for when the stash ran low. Every few miles, cruising along Highway 110, I'd toss one of the .380 shells out the window. By the time I reached Atotonilco, they were all gone.

Lost in my stoned fantasy outlaw life, I entered Bajío country and cruised along through olive and citrus groves, slowing for a couple old villages, their churches and dusty plazas hard by the roadside. I passed the birthplace of Father Hidalgo, marked on the left-hand side of the road by a tall column with a bust of the rebel priest. Two miles later, I entered Abasolo, a tidy little village whose plaza featured another monument to Miguel Hidalgo. I took a quick detour, driving slowly around the square, looking at the improbable hero who led a ragtag army to victory in Guanajuato in 1810.

Back on the main highway just past the plaza, I spotted a sign advertising La Caldera Spa, extolling the salubrious benefits of its miraculous mineral water. The turnoff to the resort was a dirt road a bit further along on the left. What sort of spa could be hidden here in the middle of rubesville?

Outside Abasolo, the countryside became broad swaths of irrigated alfalfa punctuated by prosperous redbrick farmhouses. The crop had blossomed. A profusion of tiny lavender flowers shimmered like silk as the wind sent rippling waves through the surrounding fields. Everything looked so pleasant yet dark thoughts intruded into the tranquil scenery. Killing a man infected my mind. Murder cast a long shadow. It marked you for life. The Elizabethans branded felons or cut off their ears. Behold this man. He is a murtherer. Let it come down, I thought.

I approached Irapuato. The fields here, far as the eye could see, were dense with strawberry plants. Irapuato looked to be a drab, dusty place even if it was the strawberry capital of Mexico. I turned left at the traffic circle and took a one-way street all the way through to the plaza. Coming to a Y intersection onto Highway 45, the main road between Ciudad Juárez and the Federal District, I turned left in the direction of León. Before reaching Silao, a turnoff on the right led toward Guanajuato and I was back on 110 again. Linda and I had lived in San Miguel de Allende for a month in 1962. We talked often of a bus trip to Guanajuato, only sixty miles away. For some reason, we never got around to it.

At quarter past six, I drove the final twelve miles, descending into the narrow gorge cradling the historic city between sere treeless mountains. The setting sun slanted behind me onto clustered pastel buildings, setting them alight like a cubist painting. As I drove closer the town fell into shadow. Only the church towers remained sun-gilded, gaudy with the day's demise.

Funneling down through ever-narrowing streets, Highway 110 became Juárez, the principal thoroughfare. Almost every Mexican town had a main drag named for Benito Juárez. The colonial buildings pressed in from either side. The place was enclosed, claustrophobic. Juárez carried me past the Jardín Reforma and the Plaza de la Paz. Traffic was sparse but the narrow streets threatened congestion at every intersection. Aimless pedestrians wandered in front of me with deerlike innocence.

A blast of sunlight when the pinched thoroughfare opened onto a plaza. The Teatro Juárez loomed off to my right across from the surprisingly small Jardin de la Unión. Surrounded by pink-and-blue tiled pavement, the plaza was enclosed within topiary trees clipped to form a single perfect triangle. I knew the Posada Santa Fé waited somewhere along the perimeter but couldn't see it. Several cars parked, nose forward, alongside the theater's columned portico. No sign of the red Firebird. I wasn't surprised and saw no other public parking. Linda and Nick might have been anywhere among the strollers gathering for the evening *paseo*.

In a moment, I was past the plaza, twisting through a maze of unfamiliar streets, all too narrow for parking. Hopelessly lost, I took each turn as it came, hoping pure dumb luck might return me to familiar territory. I found myself on a street called Paseo Madero, passing along a park I soon learned was called the Jardín Embajadoras. Up ahead on the corner I spotted what appeared to be an old hacienda. The sign said Motel de las Embajadoras.

I pulled over, locked the van, and went into a courtyard that made the motel look like a country inn. Several gnarled trees grew around a splashing fountain. A radio played opera somewhere in the distance. Potted plants stood everywhere. Climbing geraniums twined up the posts along the veranda where numbers of wooden cages hung, alive with birdsong.

Nosing around, I found the *patrón* in his kitchen listening to *Rigoletto* as he fried tortillas. He turned out to be an American, a pleasant energetic fellow who rented me a room for fifty pesos without meals. A week ago, this would have seemed outrageously overpriced. Now, having such a safe haven struck me as a bargain at any price. The kind of romantic place Linda would enjoy. I wondered if I would ever get her back.

The man asked where I was from "back home." I fed him a few lies as we traded tales of the expatriate life. I paid in advance. When the *patrón* gave me my room key, I told him I had no idea where I was. The man chuckled amiably. "*No problema*," he said with a wink, producing a small detailed Guanajuato street plan. He pointed to the motel's location and gave me directions to the center of town in Spanish. It was a shared joke. We weren't north of the border anymore.

My room had a dark ox-blood tile floor and colonial-style wooden furniture. I carried in Shank's satchel and my duffel, going back for the ice chest and the little net hammock bulging with fruits and vegetables. I uncapped a Pacífico and flopped on the bed, propping pillows behind me. Visions of Shank slumped like a discarded scarecrow crowded out any peace of mind. I reached for the little cigar tin in my shirt pocket. When in doubt, burn some weed.

I'd never been paranoid about smoking in Mexican hotel rooms before, but this was the first time I'd ever killed anyone. Not counting what I couldn't remember. Murder gives everything a new twist. I went back out to the VW and got the orange-crate full of canned goods and kitchen provisions, making double-sure to relock. We'd bought a box of Caracol mosquito repellent in San Blas. I unwrapped one of the green discs, carefully separating it into a continuous spiral, and balanced it on the little folding tin stand that came in the package. A thumbing of my Zippo set the serpentine coil smoldering.

Thickening clouds of astringent smoke filled the room. I set fire to the last dorf in my can. Linda and I burned Chinese joss stick incense in Frisco to disguise the pungent aroma of pot, a common hippie ploy not unknown to the fuzz and probably even more obvious in Mexico where such exotic fragrances remained unfamiliar. The acrid fumes of Caracol, a commonplace household insecticide, would arouse no undue suspicion even if mosquitoes were not a problem in Guanajuato. What would an ignorant gringo know about local insects?

I sat back on the bed, toking on the joint between sips of beer. The first happy buzz set my thoughts racing away from death but a cold, hard truth troubled me. I didn't know what to do next. All that mattered was Linda. In spite of all I'd heard, I still wanted to believe she was Nick's prisoner, held against her will. I felt ready to fight for her. Shank had been armed. I assumed Nick wore a gun and imagined facing him down with the Beretta. It felt great fantasizing about pumping him full of lead. Reality set in. Knowing now how easily these things went wrong, I needed to be very careful. No worse nightmare than accidentally shooting my wife while trying to rescue her.

If Linda was Nick's willing partner, nothing much to be done about that. To hell with begging her to come back. She'd hate it if I made a scene. I'd act noble, showing no emotion like a proper gentleman. All I wanted was a chance to say good-bye.

I pulled the Beretta from Shank's satchel and considered how to carry it concealed. The lanyard ring got me thinking about an old pair of rawhide bootlaces in my toolkit. With the ends tied together, I'd have a loop long enough to hang the automatic around my neck under my shirt. On second thought, this didn't seem so practical. I'd have to unbutton my shirt to get at the gun. I slipped the Beretta inside the waistband of my jeans behind my back, shirttails hiding the piece. This felt like a better option. I could reach around and seize the grip in a second. After a few practice tries, I started feeling like Wild Bill Hickok.

It grew dark outside the single window. A gray world turning slowly black. I stuck my head out the door to taste the coming night. The chill air felt brisk and clean. Wearing a coat in such weather would not look out of place. I dug my faded denim jacket from the bottom of the duffel and slipped it on. It had two deep inside pockets. The automatic fit nicely into the left side, butt angled for an easy draw.

I checked myself out in the full-length mirror on the inside of the *guardarropa* door. No way to tell I was heeled. I played gunfighter again with my reflection, reaching into the jacket for the pistol's grip. Better not to hurry. Trying for speed caused me to fumble and slowed my draw. An easy deliberate reach provided better results. After a few tries, I had it down pat.

I pushed a full clip into the Beretta, not cocking it but leaving the safety off. The weapon slid into my inside pocket easy as a liar's smile. I picked up my wallet and the street map, turned off the lights, locked the door, and headed uptown. It was a pleasant night fragrant with frangipani. I found my way to a street called Sangre de Christo. Guanajuato possessed a timeless quality, winding cobbled lanes and pastel houses plucked from an earlier age. Flowers grew everywhere, in tubs, pots, and windowboxes, twisting up porch columns, poking through cracks in the sidewalk. Many brightly painted wooden birdcages hung in open windows. Not a single neon sign in the entire town.

I made it up to the Jardin de la Unión in about fifteen minutes. It was seven forty-five. Well-groomed young men with freshly laundered clothes and gleaming hair gathered around the plaza for the coming *paseo*. A middle-aged guy playing an accordion sauntered past. I strolled into the triangular park searching for a sidewalk restaurant with a view of the entrance to the Posada Santa Fé. The sculpted Indian laurel trees enclosing the little space made it difficult to see out.

I cut through the heart of the tiny plaza where a brass band played on a filigreed cast-iron *quiosco*. A ring of lights around the kiosk roof gave it the look of a stationary carousel. A fountain nearby dazzled with reflected light, the play of falling water a gentle counterpoint to the martial music. Family groups and tourists clustered on ornate green benches. Their upturned eyes glittered with the merry-go-round light. A little boy wandered around the bandstand, a hollow bamboo pole angled over one shoulder. Holes drilled into the upper end were studded with cherry-red candy apples speared on sticks. It looked like an exotic plant from another planet.

I came out on the opposite side where the overhanging topiary enclosure had been trimmed away to accommodate a belle epoque lamppost and walked to the apex of the park's triangle past several sidewalk restaurants. The Posada Santa Fé stood straight ahead, a row of hotel dining tables set along the pavement under a green awning thrusting from the pink facade. The clipped cubistic trees surrounding the plaza reached across the street to the sidewalk in front of the two-story hotel. I backed away as if from a fire. Some instinct warned me not to go any closer.

Warm light spilled from a small cantina near the end of the block. I took a table with an open view of the posada's entrance. A waiter closed in. I ordered a shot of *añejo* and a bottle of Negra Modelo. A dark beer to suit my mood. I'd come all this way to learn the truth. Having it so near at hand made me doubt I could face it.

The waiter returned carrying a small tray. He set down the tequila, a saucer with lime wedges, and a tall chilled glass into which he carefully poured the beer. *"La crema de las cervezas,"* he said as the thick head formed. Making it seem like an afterthought, he placed two small snack bowls on the table. *"Mucho gusto,"* he said with practiced formality, marking my order on a scrap of brown paper before departing.

I knocked back the *añejo* and sucked on a lime wedge. Remembering to take my penicillin, I downed the pill with a swallow of beer. The bowls contained *pepitas* and fried *gusanos de maguey*. I nibbled a few salty pumpkin seeds. The crispy maggots were considered a delicacy in Mexico. I wondered if the waiter brought them as a gringo taunt.

What the hell. I reached for a handful of *gusanos*. Not all that bad. Crunchy texture. A taste of burned chocolate. When the waiter returned, the little bowl was empty.

"¿Qué le gustaría?" he inquired.

I asked for another round and inquired if the bar served anything other than snacks. The waiter said they had a nice veal stew tonight. It sounded perfect. I ordered a bowl.

"Momentito," I called as the man turned away, *"más gusanos, por favor."* The waiter cracked a brief smile.

The drinks and fried larva came first with a freshly chilled glass for the beer. I sipped my tequila, skipping the lime. The waiter brought the stew and a plate of warm tortillas wrapped in a red-checked cloth napkin. He noted the half-empty maggot bowl. *"Los gusanos fritos para una pinga más fuerte!"* he said, marking my order on the brown paper.

"Claro que sí," I replied. I was all for a ramrod dick.

The waiter winked, a fellow conspirator in the macho world of hard-ons. I tucked into the veal stew, using a folded tortilla as a supplementary spoon. Eating took the edge off my anxiety. If a stiff prick had no conscience, a full stomach owned no fear. That's why they feed you so well before the hanging.

I mopped-up the stew with my last tortilla and called for *la cuenta.* There was no formal bill. While the waiter added-up the marks on his brown paper scrap, I flipped my lucky silver Olympic coin, over and over, thinking about Linda. She loves me. She loves me not. She loves me . . .

After settling the tab, I wandered into the park finding comfort in the concealing shadows. Stealth suited my mood. Darkness seeped within. I became one with the night. Beneath the topiary trees, ghostly trunks whitewashed in lime, I felt lost to the world around me. One more ghost forgotten by the living.

Shadowed by the laurels, I stared straight at the entrance of the Posada Santa Fé. Not another soul in sight. The evening *paseo* was under way behind me within the darker confines of the park. I watched spiffy young men strutting clockwise around the plaza. Painted and coiffed *coquetas* strolled with insolent indifference in the opposite direction. They all paraded under the observant gaze of their attendant families. No one knew I was there. Alone in the dark, I felt invisible.

I pulled a dorf from my little cigar tin. A momentary

caution gave me pause. I placed it between my lips. Isolated, immune from the outside world, I flicked my Zippo and sucked down a first long toke of mota. Fragrant clouds of reefer drifted out from under the Indian laurel trees. No one noticed. Perhaps the aroma of marijuana was so familiar in the Jardín de la Unión it attracted less attention than the perfume wafting from the teenage virgins on parade. Nothing gave the invisible man away. Not smoking dope in the park nor the deafening echo of a shotgun blast in a locked hotel room.

All at once, I saw them, walking arm-in-arm toward me along the narrow sidewalk. Linda wore her favorite fringed magenta shawl. She was smiling, happy as a girl on her first date. Her amber hair gleamed in the golden light of the streetlamp. I couldn't make out what she said as they passed in front of me. Nick wore a lightweight black sateen jacket. As they headed away from my hiding place in the shadows, I saw the words *Touch of Evil* stitched in script across his back.

A novocaine numbness tingled through me. Dreading everything, I left the hiding place for my moment of truth. Nick and Linda paused outside the Posada Santa Fé, not seeing me coming. He pulled her into his arms and they kissed, long and hard, oblivious to the passing world. It hit me like a kick in the stomach. I felt the blood drain from my head, growing cold as an ambulatory corpse. Transfixed, I stared at them as they broke from their tight embrace. They entered the hotel laughing, unaware that I watched only yards away.

I wanted to follow them inside. Make a big scene in the lobby. Anything to burst the poisonous bubble welling up from deep in my soul. Fantasies of Linda held captive now seemed the most pernicious of sick jokes. Every fiber of my being screamed in pain. They were lovers. I felt like a goddamn fool and skulked off into the night.

I had no idea where to go and found myself walking along a winding lamp-lit street. Right away, I stumbled into another plaza, the surrounding buildings solid and impressive as banks. A large cathedral, another sort of bank, stood at the base of the triangular plaza. A small crowd clustered at the center by the Monumento a la Paz listening to a guitar and cello duo. The night trilled with Vivaldi.

I skirted the edges of the crowd. Music didn't do the trick. An old Indian woman sat on the church steps beside a multi-level birdcage, her iron-gray hair in long twin braids. A ragtag collection of locals stood around her. Veering away from the musicians, I strolled over for a closer look. She wore a Zapotec *huipil*. Probably traveled up from Oaxaca. Long way from home just like me. She reached inside her homemade cage. One of the fat yellow flock perched on her outstretched finger.

The Indian woman brought the bird out, and it hopped to the edge of a peculiar angled tabletop painted like a carnival game of chance with even slotted rows holding tiny paper scrolls. The little bird hopped up and down at random. After a zigzag passage, it plucked a slip from its compartment. The bird fluttered back onto the woman's forefinger. She took the rolled paper from its bill, handing it to a shy man draped in a woven woolen serape.

"*Gracias,*" he muttered, taking his secret document away

to read in private. The Indian woman returned the bird to its cage. She was a *bruja,* a fortune-telling Zapoteca witch.

"*¿Cuánto?*" I asked.

"*Un peso.*"

I dug deep in my pocket and came up with a couple *testóns.* When I handed over the fifty-centavo pieces, the woman reached into the Victorian cage. Another yellow bird jumped onto her inviting finger. The little creature bobbed across the tilted tabletop, crisscrossing with alarming determination. Pause. Head tilted. A deft peck of the beak. The yellow bird pulled a message free and returned to its master's waiting hand. I took the rolled paper into a pool of lamplight:

Un corazón roto puede arreglarse mañana;
un alma roto, nunca.

I read it over twice. "A broken heart can be fixed tomorrow; a broken soul, never." Better fortunes came in Chinese cookies. Was my heart broken? I felt betrayed, sick to my stomach. At the very deepest level, I still loved Linda. My unbroken heart was hers forever. I perceived an eternal truth. Love had nothing to do with possession. If she wanted to be with someone else, I had to let her go. I rolled the paper fortune into a ball, tossed it into the gutter and wandered up the Avenida Juárez, nursing my pain with bogus philosophy.

I found my way into the Plazuela de San Fernando, a cobbled open space with a fountain spouting at its center. Stumbling on, not caring where I was going, wanting only to get far away from where I'd been, a narrow street carried me into yet another plaza. What sort of magical city was this? Guanajuato hid as many surprises as Florence or Prague, one secluded civic playground leading to the next.

A ceramic wall plaque identified the Plaza de San Roque. The namesake church stood high on my right, a slab-sided unadorned eighteenth-century structure with a squat bell tower instead of the usual grandiose outreach to heaven. Twin stairs arched from the cobbled plaza to join together at the church entrance. I stared at the humble facade, stucco peeling from the bare brick underneath, plain as a Quaker meeting hall.

A fair-size crowd had gathered in front of the church. I edged through for a closer look. A play was in progress. Again, I felt transported into the illusion of living in another time. A half-dozen young men and women swirled before me, costumed in the manner of seventeenth-century Commedia dell'arte. "¿Qué es esto?" I asked a youthful guy standing beside me. He had the look of a student.

"Un entremés," he answered.

I didn't quite understand. An entremés was an hors d'oeuvre. Maybe this was the title of the play. The Appetizer. Perhaps it was a generic term for a type of comic sketch. I watched a pantomime sex farce. All the stock characters made an appearance. The coquette Columbine, her sad-faced white-clad husband, Pierrot, and the viejo, Pantalone. She flirted with roguish Scaramouche until nimble Harlequin came cart-wheeling out from the shadows clad in patchwork motley. Assisted by his beak-nosed sidekick, Punch the hunchback, Harlequin courted Columbine. She coyly resisted until an enormous spring-loaded phallus burst through Harlequin's parti-colored trousers.

The crowd howled with laughter. Columbine strolled off with her new beau, stroking his gigantic boner. Punch crowned the hapless weeping Pierrot with a towering pair of gilded horns. "*¡Cornudo . . . ! ¡Cornudo . . . !*" the audience jeered in unison. I stood staring, grim and mirthless.

It felt like the entire plaza was laughing at me. I pushed back through the gathered spectators and escaped into the night, hearing an echo of their savage merriment many blocks away. The derisive shouts of "*¡Cornudo!*" followed me through the darkness. Cuckold! Cuckold!

The way back to the motel was all downhill. Same direction my life was headed. I had the narrow streets to myself and would have grabbed a taxi if I'd seen one. Reaching the upper end of the Jardin de la Unión, I saw numerous *paseantes* strolling flirtatiously. I paused, dreading the possibility of bumping into Linda and Nick. To play it safe, I crossed over to the little street running along the side of the Iglesia de San Diego. I thought about going inside. As a kid, I often sat alone in the silent gothic emptiness of Grace Church before walking home from school, trying to make sense of my father's death. San Diego's gilded baroque altar with its gaudy promise of paradise put me off.

I circled around behind the church and walked toward my motel. Went out of way my to avoid running into Nick and Linda. I didn't exactly fear a confrontation; the timing just wasn't right. My wounds too fresh. When I faced them, it would be on my own terms. I needed to get my shit together.

I returned to my room a little after eleven. Walking along the deserted lamplit streets had calmed my nerves. Guanajuato was the sort of charming town Linda loved. Coming here must have been her idea not Nick's. It tormented me to see her so happy with him. I lit another Caracol and torched a dorf. With a beer dripping from the cooler and my tequila bottle on the bedside table, I sat back against a couple pillows piled up on the carved headboard.

I didn't want to think about Linda and Nick in bed across town at the Posada Santa Fé. My morbid demons imagined them fucking, bringing on spasms of intolerable pain. I couldn't get the explicit image out of my mind, returning to it again and again, like probing a chancre sore with my tongue. Did Pierrot picture Columbine doing it doggy-style with Harlequin?

This was a sucker's game. I swigged slugs of Herradura to numb the suffering. Booze and weed took the edge off my pain, but the injury continued to bleed. Cauterizing the wound, I dragged myself back, memory by memory, into the past.

I met Linda for the first time in the summer of 1960. At the Gaslight, a basement coffee house on MacDougal Street, where I'd just heard a beat poet named John Brent read his long comic epic, *Bibleland*. I spotted her leaning against the brick wall by the door. She looked like an incognito fashion model, her shabby Aquascutum raincoat and lank wet fulvous hair disguising a pre-Raphaelite beauty. When she left, I followed her up the steps out into the warm June drizzle.

"All that caffeine and culture calls for a real drink," I said, catching her eye.

Incredibly, she let me take her hand and guide her next door into the Kettle of Fish, a bar where Jack Keruoac once got the shit kicked of him. I remembered she ordered scotch on the rocks, which struck me as very sophisticated. I guzzled beer straight from the bottle. She was six months older, a Virgo with her moon in Sagittarius and Venus rising. These aspects offset her earthbound perfectionist nature and made my arty Piscean daydreams seem attractive.

Linda was in the city to take a couple political science summer courses at the New School for Social Research and lived in some posh women-only residence hotel. She planned on going to law school in hopes of an eventual career in the Foreign Service. Her wealthy Fairfield, Connecticut, family encouraged her ambitions. She said her retired brigadier general father worked as some kind of big shot at G.E. Linda was dating a Yalie at the time, a junior she bragged would be tapped for Skull and Bones next fall. I said that sounded about as much fun as being drafted into the accounting corps of the Norwegian army. She laughed. Her irreverent sense of humor gave me a foot in the door.

Linda also had a bad case of what the French called *nostalgie de la boue.* Her strong attraction to the lower depths of life was very good news for me. I soon became her prize Village gutter tramp always ready to romp in the mud. Linda felt drawn to any unfamiliar scene. That first night after leaving the Kettle, I took her over to the Five Spot to hear Ornette Coleman play free jazz on his white plastic alto sax. Much to my surprise, she dug the cacophonous quartet.

We started seeing each other nearly every night, exploring the magic back streets west of Sheridan Square where 150-year-old brick houses glowed in the light of old-fashioned cast-iron shepherd's crook street lamps. I took her to all my favorite joints. We eavesdropped on Gregory Corso and Norman Mailer at the San Remo, sang along with the bums at Sammy's Bowery Follies, and got totally plastered at the White Horse Tavern. Dylan Thomas knocked back his last whiskey there, all eighteen of them. After learning it had once been a speakeasy, Linda loved Chumley's, a dive without a sign to mark its nondescript entrance. She'd strike up a conversation with the biggest bad-ass in the joint. I dug her fearlessness and crazy sense of fun.

We didn't see each other much during the daytime except on weekends. Linda had her New School classes on West 12th Street. I worked a cool summer job at the *Village Voice*, doing paste-ups, running errands, and serving as Jules Feiffer's occasional assistant, all for a buck-ten an hour. In the fall, after returning to NYU, I hoped to keep the job part-time. I learned more at the *Voice* than in any of my comp lit courses. Every day seemed a blast in the shabby offices near Mom's apartment on Greenwich Avenue. All sorts of whacko Village characters might wander in at any moment, writers and artists hoping to get published even if they didn't get paid.

Growing up on the streets of the Village gave me an edge. Most of the old-timers knew me by sight or remembered my dad. I met both Joe "Professor Seagull" Gould and Maxwell Bodenheim in Jack Delaney's when I was eight or nine. They'd come in and cadge change for drinks, selling handwritten scraps of poetry. Dad didn't seem to mind. Said it was good for business. "People expect to see these bohemian characters when they come to the Village," he told me.

Working as the gofer at the *Voice* provided an unexpected fringe benefit. Access to the hippest parties in the Village. There were no invitations. Being in the know was all it took. When I showed up with Linda on my arm, heads turned in the smoky, crowded rooms. The jaws of the most laid-back, cooler-than-thou hipsters gaped like squares going "Wow!" at the sight of a bearded beatnik. Her cover girl features and drop-dead figure grabbed their "high intangibles." Among this tribe of drab, stringy-haired, unshaven Village chicks, Linda radiated class. She stood out in the rumpled black-clad beat crowd like a swan among crows.

I turned Linda on to her first joint at a party in a basement apartment on Perry Street, the only place in New York I knew that had a dirt floor. Don't think she even got high that first time. Along with offering weed and cheap jug wine, these parties provided a place to make out. Deep passionate kisses, pressed against the rough brick walls of some stranger's studio. Drunken fumbling feel-ups on backroom mattresses heaped with duffle coats, ponchos, and leather jackets. Kissing in a crowded loft one unseasonably cool rainy night early in July, Linda whispered, "Isn't there someplace we can be alone?"

My heart jumped a hurdle. Taking her back to my mother's apartment was impossible, and no way Linda could bring me to her cloistered residence. Out-of-towners always booked a hotel room. Someone at the *Voice* had mentioned the Hotel Earle, a cheap place popular with traveling musicians and I led Linda over to the nine-story building on Waverly Place. The rate was $3.50 for a single and five bucks double occupancy. We checked into room 707, which seemed a lucky number. "Just like the airliner," Linda said.

The little room had a nice view of Washington Square Park, wet with rain, sparkling below as we stood at the window staring into the night. I had my arms around Linda's waist, nuzzling her downy neck. She took my hands and drew them up under her thin cashmere sweater to her lace-covered breasts. Turning her head, Linda kissed me, a teasing tongue flicker as I reached behind her back to unhook her brassiere.

"Give me a minute," she whispered. My eager fingers found her puckering nipples. "I have to put in my diaphragm."

Linda slid from our embrace, snatched her Etienne Aigner shoulder bag from the floor, and disappeared into the bathroom. I undressed quickly and pulled back the covers, sliding into bed with turbocharged anticipation. I admired the calm efficient way Linda took matters in hand. If she had the diaphragm in her purse, she'd planned in advance for this moment. I fancied myself the bold seducer when all the while I was the one being seduced.

After an interminable five-minute eternity, the bathroom door opened and Linda swept naked toward me through the half light, her astonishing beauty masked by shadows.

"Knock, knock . . ." she crooned, gliding in beside me.

"Who's there?" I folded her in my arms.

"*Amore.*"

"*Amore* who?

"*Amore* know you," she breathed on my ear, "*amore* want you."

The next morning, drowsy from lack of sleep and glowing with the delicious exhaustion of marathon lovemaking, we held each other as the rising sun angled into our room. Our sporadic conversation, interrupted by muted kisses and gentle stroking, took on a new intimacy unfamiliar as the seismic contact of our naked flesh.

Linda told me she got her diaphragm not long after losing her virginity to the Yalie the night after the big game with Harvard the previous fall. I don't know why learning this stung the way it did considering I had my own cherry popped at sixteen by a Café Rienzi coffee house waitress twice my age. I had no cause for complaint. Still, the thought of some nameless blueblood twit having sex with the woman I loved rankled me. A dog's hackles always rise at the scent of a rival.

After that first night, it grew impossible to spend any time apart. We booked into the Earle with increasing frequency. Around the first of August, I shelled out twenty-five dollars and rented room 707 for a month. Linda and I didn't exactly set up housekeeping. We both had separate daytime lives. Only now we got to sleep together every night and eat dinner at one of the local restaurants and grab the cups of coffee we called breakfast in the mornings.

Her Yalie was off in England for the summer with his parents, checking out Oxford and Cambridge as potential graduate schools. By early fall, when the MV *Britannic* docked again at Pier 92 on the Hudson's luxury liner row, the lacrosse-playing jock was history. So was the boat he cruised in on. The *Britannic* sailed for the last time in December to the Scottish shipbreakers. At least that's what Linda told me with a big laugh when we got together in the city over Christmas break.

Drunk and stoned. Daydreaming about the past felt very nice when real life looked so grim. My future had as much promise as pigs in a slaughterhouse. I was a guy on the lam from a couple murders. I just found my runaway wife in another man's arms. To escape from bleak reality all I had to do was dream, dream, dream. I must have dozed off. The next thing I knew, it was dawn. I woke up fully clothed with the cold dead stub of a dorf clenched between my stained fingers.

EASTER
WEDNESDAY

— • ● • —

Blinking at the early light seeping between the curtains, I struggled to bring my new day into focus, wishing I'd just awakened from my tawdry nightmare life. No such luck. Happy endings not in my cards this hand. Tequila crashed inside my skull like a Lower Slobovian demolition derby. The bottle was two-thirds gone. I wanted a beer. Worse, I needed a beer. Just one. No way I'd hold the line at a single *cerveza*. Be drunk before noon. Not a good idea. I wanted to be sober when I confronted Linda and Nick.

Passing out meant not changing my bandage last night. I peeled off the crusty gauze pad, pleased to see the wound nicely healing. If only hearts mended so fast. After a shower and a shave, I taped on a clean gauze pad and dressed, wearing my last fresh Hawaiian shirt. I didn't have it in me to brew a pot of coffee and went in search of some joe. Spotting a light in the kitchen across the courtyard, I stumbled over the uneven paving stones, weaving between a jungle of potted plants.

I found the American proprietor hard at work tending his simmering pots. A cherubic Mexican woman assisted him, shaping tortillas by hand and frying them the old-fashioned way on a domed iron *plancha.*

"Looking a little green around the gills, *hombre,*" he said after our *buenos días* exchange.

I confessed to a wicked hangover, asking if it was too early for something to eat.

"Light's on, chow's on," the gringo *patrón* said. "Good strong coffee'll fix you right up. There's some *menudo* left over from yesterday. Best damn hangover cure known to man. Hot bowl of that and some of Esperanza's fresh tortillas, you'll be good as new."

He sat me down at a rough plank table in the corner with a steaming mug of *café con leche.* A large clay bowl of tripe stew enhanced by a squeeze of lime followed. I dipped tortillas into the stew as I ate. They were delicious, hot, and slightly charred from the griddle. The owner went about his business.

No pointless questions just to be polite. When he wasn't looking, I swallowed my meds.

I thought about what to say to Linda. Good-bye and good luck. No strings attached. I'd tell Nick I wished them well. Forget about hard feelings. Jealousy was a loser's handicap. Keep everything low-key and conversational. Ask Nick who killed Frankie when he wasn't expecting the question. Catch him off-guard. Get the truth out of him and be on my way.

I wolfed down the *menudo*. By the bottom of a second mug of coffee, I felt a fighting chance for life beyond pain. Linda was an early riser. Knowing Nick liked to sleep in, I figured she'd go along with the program. I wanted to catch them at a disadvantage. An unexpected visit. If they were still in bed, so much the better. A guy was less inclined to act tough with no pants on.

I took my last sip of java, paid the *patrón* for another day and asked about the best place to catch a cab. "*Aqui, amigo,*" he replied. "I'll phone one for you." I said I'd wait in my room.

Walking back across the courtyard, the morning sun felt warm on my bare arms, a pleasing contrast with the chill mountain air. By noon, it'd be too hot for a coat. I slipped on my denim jacket anyway, the Beretta's weight thumping against my hip. I considered leaving the gun behind. Nick always came off as a decent guy but hung out with filth like Shank. Better to be prepared. An outlaw Boy Scout.

The *taxista* knocked on my door. I told him the Jardin de la Unión. He said okay. Three minutes later, the driver dropped me off in front of the Teatro Juárez. I crossed the blue-tiled plaza to the Posada Santa Fé. Linda and Nick wouldn't be registered under their real names. I worked it out in my mind how to ask for them.

The hotel lobby looked more splendid than expected. Tiled floors, arches, exposed ceiling beams, wall murals, everything evoking wealth and power in a retro-conquistador style. At the front desk, I told the clerk I'd come to see my sister and her boyfriend, describing Linda and Nick as best I could. The clerk knew just whom I was talking about. The *"pareja feliz"* had gone out together about half an hour earlier. Hearing them called a "happy couple" felt like getting mugged.

"¿Adónde iban?" I asked.

"Están visitando las momias."

"¿Que?"

"Las momias," he repeated, showing me a postcard on the desktop rack depicting twin rows of desiccated cadavers lined against either side of what looked to be some sort of tunnel. I plucked the card from the display and turned it over to read the caption on the reverse. *Momias* were mummies. Looking again at the picture, I saw an arched room at the end of the tunnel stacked floor to ceiling with human skulls. I paid him for the postcard and asked where I could find the mummies.

"Al panteón de Santa Paula," he replied.

"Gracias," I said and walked back out onto the street, studying the macabre postcard. I thought about returning and asking the deskman to call for a cab when one pulled up out front, disgorging a load of middle-aged American tourists. Two loud couples, pink and patriotic, chattering like chipmunks.

I waited while the driver wrestled their suitcases from the trunk, climbing into the backseat only when he received the gringos' payment.

"*Ah, sí,*" he said when I asked him to take me to the *panteón.*

"*Las momias,*" I added.

"*Sí, sí . . . todo el mundo quiere ver las momias.*"

I made no reply. If the whole damn world wanted to see the mummies, why had I never heard of them until today?

I stared at the postcard as the cab wound up a steep cobbled street, thinking of taxidermy frog bands, border town novelties, amphibian carcasses inflated and shellacked, each round shiny mounted musician holding a carved wooden guitar, fiddle, saxophone, or trumpet. The corpses on the card weren't plump and gleaming like the frogs but conjured a similar macabre show biz image. A chorus line of death, tattered, wrinkled, frozen in a final synchronized kick step. Mummified "Rockettes" dancing in a phantom pharaoh's tomb.

We pulled to a stop outside. The red Pontiac was parked by the churchyard wall. No other vehicles in sight. Poised eternally for a flight never to come, carved stone angels veiled in bird droppings stood on each corner of the thick adobe enclosure. Noting my distraction, the driver demanded an insane fare. "*Cinco pesos,*" I said. "*Nada más.*"

The man grinned, accepting the five, asking if I needed a ride down the hill after visiting the *panteón.* I said I preferred to walk and he drove off. An open gate framed scrolled-ironwork calligraphy forged by a master blacksmith. I stepped inside among the tombstones. More tilted stone angels brooded over lost memories amid a grove of marble crosses. Vaults stacked like filing cabinets lined the inner walls, marble plaques identifying the remains housed within. Some stood empty, rude brick interiors exposed like gutless cadavers in the anatomy lab.

A couple old men fussed about a grave in a corner of the churchyard. One pushed a wheelbarrow. The other walked with a cane and gave the orders. The little church looked modest next to the gaudy mausoleums encircling it. Carved into the lintel above a door, I read VENIO A MI HIJOS MIOS. Come to me, my sons, I thought, wishing such a refuge was really possible. Close by the church wall, a tomb with an open wooden hatch invited a closer look. I found a circular opening into the earth. A set of stone steps corkscrewed into darkness.

Dreading the descent, I hesitated at the silent spiral and removed my sunglasses, tucking them into my shirt pocket before starting down, one silent step at a time. The stairs wound out into a long vaulted whitewashed crypt twenty feet deep in the ground, lighted at either end by semicircular clerestory windows. It smelled damp and earthy. No trace of the expected rot. The place was a sanctuary for oblivion.

I studied the postcard trying to get my bearings. This was not the room with the mummies. A number of arched vaults fifteen feet deep gaped in a row along the wall to my right. The first few appeared empty. I couldn't tell about those farther down. Back when the postcard photo was taken, these little caverns were stacked high with skulls. Using the card as my guide, I found the open beveled glass double-doors at the far end of the nave. The entrance to the hall of the mummies.

I crept along the arching crypt, silent in my Converse high-tops, stopping a yard or so from the open glass doors, listening for any conversation. Hearing only silence, I took two deft steps and peered around the corner. Linda and Nick stood inside, their backs toward me. Not holding hands or talking or anything. Just staring at the far end of the vaulted tunnel. On either side, twin rows of corpses looked on, a silent audience of the dead.

I ducked back out of sight. Nick wore his black Hollywood crew jacket and a goofy straw planter's hat. Linda had on a red floral-printed Marimekko dress, the sleeves of a light pink cardigan sweater tied around her neck, her shoulder bag hanging from a strap. No telling what Nick might have hidden under his coat. Be prepared. I pulled out the Beretta, drawing back the slide. Holding the little automatic at my side I stepped into the adjacent crypt.

They didn't hear me coming. The vault was nearly a hundred feet long, about like the one at my back. I walked quietly toward them past a gauntlet of the dead, gape-jawed and staring with isinglass eyes melted into tattered parchment faces. I stopped about twenty feet behind them, concealed by silence. They stared like art gallery spectators at the cadaver of a little girl in her white christening dress kneeling within a niche in the end wall. Linda and I had a private joke about how to say, "See you later, alligator," in Spanish.

"*Hasta mañana, iguana,*" I murmured.

They both turned. Linda's startled look betrayed an effort to stay cool. Nick wore shades. He broke into a big shit-eating grin. "Amigo, Tod," he said. "You've come to the right place."

"I've come to say good-bye to my wife."

"How'd you track us down?"

"Shank told me where to look."

"Now, why would he do that?"

"He planned on killing me. Guess he thought it didn't matter."

"Why didn't he?"

"Didn't he what?"

"Kill you?"

Here we go, I thought. "He died first," I said, bringing the Beretta up into view. I didn't aim at anyone, just pointed the muzzle in Nick's general direction. His smile grew a degree whiter. Linda remained expressionless, observing the proceedings with her cat-green stare.

"Lookee here," Nick said. "The Tod-man is packing. Brought a little heat to the party." Nick held the sides of his jacket open to show he had nothing hidden. "I'm clean, Tod," he said, folding his arms across his chest. "Why don't you try and relax a little bit."

"I'm plenty relaxed," I said. "Afraid I'll get nervous and shoot somebody by accident?"

"Ol' compadre, there's nothing about you that frightens me. You're the kind of punk be begging for protection in the joint. Explain to me how bad-ass old Shank came to cash in his chips this early in the game?"

"I got nervous and shot him by accident."

"Bullshit!"

"No. *Es la verdad.* Shank killed Doc. Sort of by surprise. Big surprise for Doc anyway. He didn't even have a gun. The noise made me jump and my piece went off. Had a hair-trigger."

"Shank fucked up," Nick snarled, his fake smile fading. "He should've took you out *primero*."

"His exact last words. We all make mistakes."

"Yeah . . . ? Well, you made one hell of a big mistake coming here after us. Planning on getting 'nervous' again? Jealous husband shoots two-timing wife by accident?"

I raised the automatic, aiming it straight at Nick. "Told you. I'm here to say good-bye. If that's the way Linda wants it. I'd never hurt you, honey. You know that." I looked at my reflection in Nick's mirrored lenses. "This piece of shit is another story."

"My, my, my," Nick sneered. "Tough talk from a two-bit punk." He glanced over at Linda who stared at me with a child's curiosity. "Hey, doll, tell big bad hubby to take a powder before somebody jams his popgun up his ass!"

"He's right, Tod," she said without emotion. "Best if you went right now."

"Okay. If that's what you want. I need a couple questions answered first."

"Please." Linda gave me her take-no-prisoners stare. "You have no right to ask about anything."

"Hey, relax. I don't give a shit who you shack up with. Even the Bongo King here."

"Ain't he a prince?" Nick's sardonic grin expressed only scorn. "Some kind of saint."

"One thing I need to know," I said. "Then I'll split."

"Want to know how I taught your wife to swallow?"

That hit hard. I caught my breath, choking back any wise guy reply. "No," I said. "Tell me who killed Frankie."

171

Nick grinned for real this time. "Don't you know?"

"I . . . can't remember. . . ." Nick laughed out loud. "Doc and Shank told me they didn't do it," I said. "That leaves you."

"What makes you think they told the truth?"

"I can dig it," I said, feeling the Beretta steady in my right hand. "They were both cheap, dumb, lying crooks like you."

Nick flinched. I struck a nerve. It was the bit about being dumb. Nick fancied himself a cellblock intellectual.

"Maybe you did it." Nick licked his lips. "Maybe you blocked it from your memory. Some kind of partial amnesia because your subconscious couldn't handle it." He came on pretty strong with his armchair psychology. Calling him dumb must have really stung.

"Shank and Doc said they weren't in the room when it happened."

"You were in the room when it happened," Nick growled, pulling off his aviator glasses to glare at me. "Your knife cut her throat. The one you carry around everywhere." As he spoke, I felt the sheathed Randall pressing into the small of my back. "You killed Frankie right after you fucked her." My dumbstruck expression betrayed my thoughts. "Hell, you can't even remember that? Must not have been a very good piece of ass."

"I don't know what you're talking about."

"Linda watched you two go at it like dogs in heat. Ask her if you don't believe me."

That packed a wallop. Linda stared at me without expression, a biology student dissecting a frog. "I'm sorry," I muttered. She said nothing, her keen jade eyes probing deeper into the wound. "I . . . don't remember any of it."

Nick grinned like mad now. "You're one lucky son of a bitch," he said. "No guilty conscience. No sleepless nights. You just committed the perfect murder."

"No," I blurted. "No, I didn't. I didn't kill Frankie!"

Nick scowled. "What makes you so damn sure if you can't remember a fucking thing?"

"I just know way deep down. There's no way, no way in hell, I offed Frankie. It had to be you, Nick. You killed her with my knife. Set me up to be your fall guy. I feel it in my gut, you stupid stinking sack of snake shit!"

Anger darkened Nick's dusky complexion. Hot blood flowed into his face. He changed color like an agitated tropical lizard. "*Mayate*," he hissed.

I have no idea why he called me a faggot. Maybe it was the most damning pejorative in a jailbird's lexicon. "You want to feel it in your gut? I got something'll give you a real bellyache." He looked over at Linda who remained impassive. Her feline eyes gleamed with predatory intelligence. She didn't acknowledge Nick's furious imploring glance. His glare refocused on me. "You want the truth, asshole!" he snarled. "Go ahead! Tell him the truth, Linda."

No tomb was ever more silent. Mummies frozen for all eternity grimaced on either side. Like the whole world ceased breathing, time grinding to a stop. "I did it, Tod," Linda said, breaking the funereal hush.

"What . . . ?"

"I killed Frankie."

"I don't believe you. You're covering for Nick."

"Clue him in, baby." Nick gave us his feral grin, a quick glint of canine teeth. "Blow by blow."

I stared at Linda in anguish. She met my gaze, unwavering, utterly devoid of any emotion. "It started after you shot up," she said. "Remember that?" I nodded. "I was furious with you. I've never done heroin. Never. Not even now. But you . . . You went for it like a hog eating garbage.

"Things got really crazy. Frankie stripped off all her clothes and danced naked around the room, her big fat tits flopping. 'Making the eagle fly,' she called it. She said she wanted to get laid and started screaming, 'Somebody fuck me! Somebody fuck me!' Remember that?"

"No," I mumbled, avoiding Linda's furious accusing eyes.

"How convenient. I'll never forget. I was stoned and drunk but watching you peel off your shorts and dance bare-ass with that fat whore will stay with me for the rest of my life."

"I'm sorry." I lowered the Beretta, aiming at the floor between me and Nick.

"You're *sorry*? Don't be a hypocrite. What's there to be sorry about if you can't remember anything?"

"What I . . . I . . . Never meant to hurt you."

"Little late for that. My feelings didn't mean shit to you when you jumped Frankie's bones. We all stood around the bed, laughing and cheering and clapping out the rhythm. I hated you then."

I cringed. What a creep. Fucking in front of my wife. A rat in the gutter. Not remembering didn't make it any easier to forget. "Forgive me," I pleaded. "Please."

"What for? A quick lay with some slut? Think I give a shit about that? I hate how stupid you looked passed out on top of her. Two drooling, snoring drunks covered in cum and slobber. Such a pretty sight. The life of the party."

For a fragmentary moment, I saw the brief beginnings of a smile playing on Linda's lips. Her eyes burned deep into my soul. "Too bad I missed such a good time," I said.

Linda's faint smile became a grimace. "The party was over," she said. "Doc and Shank disappeared someplace. Nick and I sat on the foot of the bed, swigging tequila. I hated you so much then. You and the *puta* snoring like Romulans. I said something about wishing you were dead. Nick said, 'Why don't you kill them? Make you feel better.'

"I was so drunk. It made perfect sense. You two were crud. Deserved to die. I asked Nick if I should bash your heads in with a hammer.

"'Too messy,' he said. 'A lady uses poison, or a dagger.'

"'Poison's too slow,' I said. Nick told me your daddy's knife was keen as a razor. There it was on the floor. On your belt. Where you'd dropped your shorts. I never knew how sharp it was.

"Frankie lay on her back, mouth wide open, making walrus noises. I wanted to kill her just to stop the snoring."

"Linda, please . . ." I pleaded. "I can't hear anymore."

"This is important, Tod," she said. "Deep down in your bargain-basement heart, I want you to know the truth." She said this without emphasis like ordering a second beer. "I took Frankie by the hair and pulled her head back. Think if she woke up then I would have stopped. She just snored on into oblivion. Your knife went through her throat so easy. Easier than carving a turkey."

I cringed at Linda's casual offhand indifference. She might have been describing brushing her teeth in the morning. "No more . . . Please," I begged.

"Wasn't much blood right away." Linda continued in her newscaster's monotone. "Just flowed out smooth as warm crimson paint. I felt some resistance, not much, nothing more than slicing a drumstick from the thigh. I cut through. Severed the cartilage. The blood gushed up then, steady, pulsing like some kind of baptism.

"Such a great feeling of control. Absolute total power. Better than sex. Frankie opened her eyes. She stared up at me. Don't know if she saw anything. The only sound was her dreadful gurgle. I thought she might scream. Cry out in some way. It's what I wanted. She only made this noise like tub water swirling down a drain."

I tried hard to say something. No words came. Linda looked at me like I wasn't really there. "Nothing noble about death," she said. "No dignity in dying. You're just a hunk of meat. All glory to the butcher. His hand holds the knife."

Linda's matter-of-fact tone made her grim confession more chilling. She might have been reciting one of her mother's recipes. B-movie maniacs and pulp fiction lunatics rave and babble. I wanted my wife to rant like some mad scientist taking over the world. Her calm deliberate narrative made insanity seem rational. That felt most frightening of all.

"Why didn't you kill me, too?" I asked, not really sure I wanted to know.

"Can't say." Linda's brow wrinkled. She had to think about it. "I wanted to. Hated you so much. Frankie's blood washed it all away. Dropped your knife on the bed. Nick said we should pack up and clear out. Made sense at the time."

"Leaving me holding the bag?"

"I didn't think of it like that. More like running away from childhood mischief. No one wants to get caught. Blaming you wasn't the point. You were passed out. I wanted you to wake up beside your fat dead whore."

"Thanks for the memories," I muttered. What more to say? Have a nice life? See you around some time? Be happy? I felt like I bid good-bye to someone I didn't know. No words for it. An awkward half-wave as I turned to leave.

"Where do you think you're going?" Nick barked at me.

"I have no idea." Looking back at them, I felt only an empty sick feeling. "Far away from the two of you as possible."

"Don't count on it," he snarled, putting his shades back on. "You're staying put right here."

"Big talk for a little man with no gun," I said.

Nick started toward me. "I don't need a fucking gun to take you down."

I raised the automatic and aimed at the middle of his chest. "Hold it right there!"

Nick paused, grinning at me, hands on his hips. "Maybe you blew Shank away by accident," he said, "but you're much too pussy to bust a cap on a man looking you in the eye." He took another step closer holding out his open palms, showing he had nothing to hide. "'Specially when he's unarmed."

"Don't do it, Nick," I warned. "Don't be stupid."

"Stupid . . . ?" He kept on coming. "Why tag a man as stupid just because he's got the *cojones* to call your bluff?"

Nick was only feet away. "Stay back," I said, hearing fear tremble in my voice. "One more step and you're dead."

He just laughed at me. "If you meant to shoot, I'd be dead

already." Nick closed the distance and grabbed my right wrist with his left hand, turning the Beretta's muzzle away. "Let go," he commanded, taking hold of the barrel with his right. I let him have the gun.

"Your lucky day," I said.

"Don't take no luck to face down a weak sister like you." He held the Beretta by the barrel, butt pointed harmlessly at me. "Trouble is, Tod, you know way too damn much. Never mind everything Linda told you. Seeing us here together is very bad news for you. Have a nice long look all around. In a minute, you'll be one of them. Just another stiff in the boneyard."

I couldn't believe I was about to die. There had to be a way to make a deal. Say the right words. Talk my way out of the whole sorry mess. Drawing a blank, I stared at the desiccated cadavers wired upright to hooks in the wall on either side. Most were naked. Not that it mattered. Male or female, their genitalia had withered into formless ancient fruit. Clothed ladies faced eternity in stained old-fashioned dresses. One bearded fellow that looked like a nightmarish wolfman had on a dusty woolen suit and vest. Another wore a faded uniform with tarnished brass buttons and epaulets. Their mouths all hung open, arrested in a final scream. The silent sound of their eternal agony filled the vaulted chamber. Like a dog attuned to frequencies high above human awareness, I heard the shrieking chorus of their endless howling. I knew at that moment I was a dead man.

"Why would I ever say anything about Frankie?" I tried buying some time. "I'm in deep as you. Hell, it's your word against mine."

"This has nothing to do with Frankie. No hard feelings, pal. Just the way it is." Nick reached back and handed the Beretta to Linda. "Go ahead," he said. "Ice him, doll."

I stared at my wife, looking deep into her eyes. Her face remained expressionless. I felt numb. No thoughts. No nothing. She raised the pistol, holding it with both hands. The muzzle pointed straight at me. A slight smile formed on her lips. She shifted her aim and shot Nick in the back of the head.

His straw hat sailed into the air as he took one stumbling step and collapsed face forward at my feet. The echo of the automatic's report reverberated in the narrow vault, a sound loud enough to annul the silent screaming of the dead. I looked at Linda, bewildered.

"Ice him," she said, her voice acid with ironic scorn. "Like some third-rate Cagney movie." Linda approached me, the pistol held slack at her side. "Can't tell you how sick I was of all that jive-ass jailhouse shit."

She stepped in close and threw her left arm around my neck, kissing me hard on the mouth. An intensity vibrated from the core of her being, a fiery comet from the far outer-reaches of passion. She bit the inside of my lip. I tasted blood. "Here," she said, handing me the Beretta as she broke from the embrace. "If somebody comes, say Nick was a stranger trying to rape me." She tugged the top of her cotton dress until the seam ripped free, exposing a bare shoulder beneath the sleeve-knotted cardigan. "We've got to hurry!"

I watched Linda run the length of the vaulted crypt and peer around the corner. Glancing at Nick, I saw surprisingly little blood. A red puncture smaller than a dime showed through his slick black hair. I felt nothing. No compassion or pity or shame. I watched as if it all happened to somebody else. Linda walked quickly back satisfied the coast was clear. Kneeling by the body, she skimmed Nick's straw hat up at me like a Frisbee. "Put it on," she said as I caught the brim. I did as told, blood tasting like pennies in my mouth.

Linda turned Nick's pockets inside out, stuffing his wallet and other junk into her shoulder bag. She pulled off his sunglasses and tugged the dying man's arms, one at a time, from his black jacket. "We've got to get him out of here," she said, rolling the coat into a tidy bundle easy as throwing away the trash. "Somewhere they won't find him for a while."

"How about down there." I pointed to the empty vaults where the skulls had once been stacked.

Linda glanced over her shoulder. "Come on," she said with a smile. "Lend a hand."

I shoved the Beretta back into my jacket pocket. We each took one of Nick's arms, dragging him face down. This proved cumbersome. After a couple yards, we turned him over onto his back. It got easier after that. I avoided Nick's startled eyes. In what seemed a hundred years, we pulled the body to the farthest, darkest empty vault.

We propped Nick up against the back wall, slumped spread-legged like a drunk. Linda checked the body one last time, stripping off his watch and a heavy gold signet ring, tugging a gold crucifix and chain from around his neck. She dropped it all into her shoulder bag. From out front, no sign of Nick could be seen in the far shadows.

"Good place for him," Linda said. "Not many people come down here. The *viejo* who let us in said we were the first visitors in a week." I recalled the cab driver's boast about the whole world wanting to see the mummies. Linda tossed me Nick's sateen coat. "Take off your jacket and put this one on. His shades, too." Again, I obeyed her command and watched as she slid her flat-soled sandals along the length of the crypt, erasing the drag marks from the dusty flagstones paving the floor.

Who was this woman I'd shared my life with for eight years? She killed Nick with less emotion than swatting a fly. Now she tidied up after the murder like Lady Macbeth on a cleaning spree. I watched her walking toward me between the ranked cadavers, savoring a copper taste of blood in my mouth, her wicked smile arousing love's high-voltage surge.

Linda pulled on her pink cardigan, concealing the torn dress. "No need for the rape story," she said. "Too bad I ruined my sheath."

"Cheap enough to fix."

"That's what I love about you." She kissed me, a quick peck on the lips. "Always so practical."

"Am I . . . ?"

"Busy, busy, busy with your toolbox. The beatnik Mr. Fix-It."

So surreal. Nick lay dead down the hall. The smell of gunpowder hung in the air. Linda and I had killed three people between us. Our mindless chatter remained unchanged. She dug deep down into the inner reaches of her shoulder bag, searching with the tactile expertise of the blind and came up with an eyebrow pencil. "Hold still," she said. "Mr. Fix-It needs a little fixing up." With a few deft strokes, Linda sketched an approximation of Nick's mustache above my upper lip. "There." She giggled. "A cross between Clark Gable and Groucho."

Linda led the way up the spiral staircase out of the claustrophobic chamber of death into the clean open air. She took my arm as we walked across the churchyard. I carried my bundled denim jacket, the Beretta wrapped inside, in my other hand. The two old men with the wheelbarrow were still at their graveside task, frozen in time. Linda gave them a friendly wave. When I attempted a broad Nick-style grin, she whispered, "Don't push your luck."

We strolled through the open gate, casual as tourists. Linda fished the car keys from her shoulder bag and unlocked the Firebird. A moment later, we drove back down the hill, our slow speed a defiant rebuke to the big V-8's throaty rumble. After less than half a mile, Linda pulled over by the side of the road.

"Better clean up your act," she said, taking a small jar of cold cream and a pocket pack of Kleenex from her purse. She gently wiped the cartoon mustache from my face. I studied her sea-green eyes, intent on their task, marveling how the color always varied depending on her mood.

"Why didn't you do it?" I asked.

"Do what? Shoot you?" Linda wiped a final trace of cold cream from my lip. "If I wanted to kill you," she said, "I would have done it in Barra."

"Much easier to pull a trigger."

"Don't be so sure." Linda smiled at me. "Accidents don't

count." She stuffed the cold cream and Kleenex back in her bag, feeling around inside. "Besides, I could have shot you the minute I saw you." Linda pulled something shiny from the depths of the leather sack. "With this."

I stared at a tiny nickel-plated automatic with mother-of-pearl grips balanced on the palm of her hand. It looked smaller than a cigarette case. "Where'd you get that?"

"It's a 'Baby' Browning," Linda said. ".25 caliber. Six shots. Nick bought it for me our first night in Guad. We'd gone to see some guy named Enrique about guns. Shank and Nick wanted bigger stuff. More firepower. Enrique said he'd handle it for them in a day or two. Shank stayed on in the city to finish the deal. He was supposed to meet us tomorrow."

"Looks like a toy. Have you ever shot it? I mean, before just now."

Linda nodded. "Nick gave me a lesson yesterday."

"Tough luck for him."

"He was an idiot. Thought he had all the angles covered." Linda shoved the little pistol back into her purse. "It was mostly talk. That's what he was good at."

She put the pony car in gear and eased back onto the cobbled road. I studied her classic profile as she drove. Hard to imagine she murdered two people in cold blood. I understood for the first time that almost anyone, any stranger in the crowd, might be a killer. This was a disturbing thought. In nature, it is easy to tell the predators from the prey. Innocent bunnies look different from savage tigers. Out in the human world, lost in the passing man swarm, nothing distinguishes the hunters from their quarry.

At the bottom of the hill, Linda turned off a side street into the large parking area in front of the railroad station. "Not a good idea for someone at the hotel to see us together," she said. "Same goes for wherever you're staying."

"Okay," I said.

"You should be able to catch a cab here pretty easy."

"Okay."

"Do you know a little town called Abasolo? About forty miles west, past Irapuato on Highway 110?"

"Drove through it yesterday."

"Great. There's a hot springs spa in Abasolo called La Caldera. Why don't we meet there later on?"

"It's a date," I said.

"Whoever gets there first books the room."

"What name should we use?"

"Ours, silly. They might ask to see our tourist cards."

"Did you give your real name at the Posada Santa Fé?"

"Sure. Hide in plain sight. Nick taught me never to break more than one law at a time."

"So damn smart he landed in San Quentin."

Linda ignored that one, responding with a slight shrug. "We better get moving," she said. "Let me have his jacket. I'm keeping it."

"What for? A souvenir?"

"Orson Welles gave it to Nick for playing bongos on the soundtrack of his movie."

"Bullshit!"

"Maybe. It's way too cool to throw away."

I peeled off the black jacket and handed it to her. "You can keep the hat," she said.

"I don't want his fucking doofus hat!"

"Just dump it somewhere." She leaned over and kissed me sweetly on the mouth. "Look. I have to go and pack. See you at La Caldera."

I climbed out, staring after the Firebird's slit rear taillights as she drove off. No taxis in sight. I pulled on my denim jacket and paced back and forth in front of the train station for about fifteen minutes. Cabs probably only came to meet the trains. I went into the waiting room to check the schedule. The next arrival wasn't due until four in the afternoon. Hanging around was a sucker's bet. After a few rudimentary directions from the man at the ticket window, I set off on foot for my motel.

Along the way, I passed the Mercado Hidalgo, the city's fifty-year-old market, big as the train station and spire-crowned by a central clock tower weathervane. I felt the pistol in my pocket. The scent of gunpowder lingered about me. Death and blood. Holy Week be damned. Canvas-topped stalls stood in rows outside the market building selling everything from tacos to plastic kitchenware. One booth stood out from the others, brilliant with cut flowers. An Indian woman tended the make-believe garden. Wanting to smell something sweet and clean, I pointed at various bouquets.

A little kid wandered over, a cardboard box bottom slung around his neck like a tray on a length of string. He sold Chiclets packaged two per tiny container. The way they came from subway platform penny-vending machines when I was in grade school. I said I didn't want any gum. His sad look made me feel for him. I tousled his black hair. "¿*Quieres un sombrero, chico?*" I asked. The kid's eyes lit up like candles on a birthday cake.

"*Sí, señor.*"

I placed Nick's straw planter's hat on the kid's head. It drooped down over his ears. "*Las gafas de sol, también,*" I said and gave him the aviator glasses. He put them on. They were way too big and hung crookedly on the bridge of his nose. The kid loved it. A cheerful *gracias*, and he rushed off to check his reflection in the nearest window.

My spontaneous generosity cost me any advantage in the bargaining. Putting my Ray-Bans back on didn't help. The flower vendor saw through my bluff. I paid her asking price and strolled off down the twisting street holding an armload of flowers.

I was still crazy in love with Linda. You'd have to be crazy to love a murderess. Only another killer with blood on his hands, accidental or not, could recognize the deep bond all assassins share. I figured she killed Nick to save my life. How could you not love someone forever for that? The debt I owed her was beyond repayment. Linda was stoned out of her mind when it happened with Frankie. Nick told her what to do. Who knows what she remembered the next day. Maybe Nick fed her a line of bull? I fucked Frankie and can't remember. Linda watched me. Crimes of passion aren't murder. Try telling that to the law. We both needed to get out of Mexico on the double.

It took an hour to walk back to the Motel de las Embajadoras. The American owner was nowhere in sight. Safe in my room with the curtains pulled, I opened a beer and ignited a dorf. I'd paid for an extra day. The bed had been made. No one would come around until the next morning. I half-filled a small plastic wastebasket with water in the bathroom, stuffing in the flowers. Searching among my writing stuff, I found an envelope and slipped a *veinte* note inside. I wrote *"por la papelera"* on the front and left it on the bed.

Packed and ready to go in twenty minutes. The Beretta went back into Shank's satchel. I had no further use for an automatic aside from its value on the black market. Stashing my gear took almost no time. I left the room key in the lock, driving off with the flowers wedged into the space in front of the passenger seat.

I drove out of Guanajuato the same way I'd come in. Up sinuous streets winding between buildings in every color of an artist's palette. Anxious to get out of town, I was pissed when a delivery truck blocked the way. It backed into an alley near the Jardin de la Unión. A kid walked alongside, beating a double tattoo on the truck's side panel, guiding it into place. A final single beat signaled the driver he'd made it. I swung out around them, easing past the Teatro Juárez.

At the top of the hill outside the city, I stopped and took a Pacífico from my cooler. Driving on Highway 110 toward Irapuato, I imagined rewinding the past, traveling backward in time, my magic car in reverse all the way to Barra, erasing the entire week as I sped along, minute by minute, mile by mile. Before long, I passed through the dusty strawberry capital again.

On the outskirts of town, little boys with torn trousers stood along the side of the road holding baskets of strawberries for sale. I'd seen them yesterday on my way to Guanajuato and sped past with something else on my mind. Today, fresh-picked sweet *fresas* seemed perfect. Succulent red fruit might purge the taste of death.

I pulled over and the three closest boys came running. They clamored loudly for my attention, lifting baskets high above their heads as I leaned out the window. Their competition didn't affect the prices. All wanted ten pesos for what looked to be about a kilo of berries. Each insisted in shrill discord with the others on the superior qualities of his own fruit. The baskets all looked about the same. I picked one at random, paid the happy urchin and drove off with my bounty.

Up until a few days ago, Linda and I had been faithful partners. Friends found our fidelity hard to believe in a free-wheeling age of sex, drugs, and rock-and-roll. We considered ourselves lucky, ignorant of crabs and the clap. A decade older than most of the hippies flooding into Frisco, our matrimonial models had been Ozzie and Harriet, that perfect TV couple, along with their comic book counterparts, Blondie and Dagwood. We learned about romance from Hollywood movies where even hip couples like Nick and Nora Charles slept in twin beds.

The pill provided the magic bullet launching the sexual revolution. For Linda and me, it became a key to freedom. No more putting in the "thing." An end to foul-tasting spermicide cream. Unexpected spontaneous moments. My mom arranged for Linda's Enovid prescription. The pill was illegal in Connecticut. Mother got her an appointment with a gynecologist in the city but still refused to let us shack up at her place.

The twenty-mile drive between Irapuato and Abasalo passed pleasantly through a purple sea of alfalfa. Stoned, I floated along enjoying the lush view. I reached Absalo in about half an hour and spotted the sign LA CALDERA SPA at the entrance to town. Turning onto a dirt road through the surrounding fields, I soon came to a large ranch, passing tile-roofed concrete hog pens and storage sheds. Beyond, several handsome buildings stood among shade trees. Steaming outdoor pools reflected the midday sky.

I saw no sign of the red Pontiac. Impossible that Linda hadn't gotten here first. She never meant to come. Was this another setup? Maybe she sold me out to the Federales? Tipped them off about where to find Nick's body. I didn't like the feel of things and thought of making a U-turn to split for parts unknown. Love calmed my paranoia. Reason demanded trust. No more acting like a panic-driven fool.

I stopped by the main building and gave my name to the clerk at the front desk. He said my wife had already arrived and was staying in room 27. He asked if I wanted my own key.

Por favor, I replied. He slid a large brass disc with a dangling key attached over to me. Parking was around back.

I drove Bitter Lemon to the rear of the building, pulling in next to the Firebird. Unloading the cooler, I set the flowers on the lid between Shank's satchel and my small duffel and locked the van. I grabbed the ice chest handles, carrying the whole lazy man's load into the resort. Room 27 was on the second floor. Water sloshed out of the wastebasket as I struggled up the stairs.

I set everything down outside the door and knocked once. Getting no answer, I turned my key in the lock. It was dim inside, curtains drawn against the searing afternoon sun. Jasmine incense and marijuana scented the closeted air. Several candles glittered, tiny winking fireflies in the artificial gloom. I hauled the cooler inside and closed the door.

For a moment, I didn't move, eyes adjusting to the darkness. Twin candles flickered on a bedside table. Linda lay naked on her back across the white chenille counterpane, watching me. Candlelight bathed her cinnamon-tanned flesh with a rosy glow. Made her copper hair gleam like molten ore. I took the bucket of flowers and walked toward the bed. "These are for you," I said.

"You're sweet." Her eyes never left mine.

"Want some strawberries?"

"I want you," she said.

I sat on the edge of the bed, setting the flowers between two bright candles illuminating the nightstand. "I'm here."

"Why are you wearing so many damned clothes?"

I peeled out of my high-tops, Levis, and Hawaiian shirt. In a heartbeat, I lost myself in her cool enfolding embrace. "*Hasta mañana, iguana,*" she whispered.

After eight years of sleeping with Linda, I thought I knew everything about her. Instead, I found myself in bed with a stranger.

The gentle lover became an unfamiliar aggressor. Grabbing me in a fierce embrace, Linda rolled me onto my back, straddling my waist and pinning my shoulders. It seemed like an assault.

She bit my neck, clawing her way down my body, scratching and nipping. My erection pulsed. I felt afraid. Linda took my swollen cock deep into her mouth, lubricating with her tongue. A breath-held heartbeat later, she forced me up between her legs. Arching her back, she rode up and down like the trained equestrian she'd been as a schoolgirl. I attempted to draw her close for a kiss. She grabbed my hands and pulled them to her breasts, holding them there as I pinched her nipples.

It was all about her pleasure. Linda remained in total control. When I felt close to climaxing, she lifted off me, turning onto her elbows and knees. I sat up, her beautifully rounded ass raised before me. She looked back over her shoulder with a savage smile. "Like lions," she commanded.

I mounted her, plunging in with forceful strokes. She cried out, "Bite me!" I seized the nape of her neck between my teeth. Linda screamed as my orgasm exploded. I heard myself gasping. We disengaged and collapsed together.

All suddenly gentle, we lay side-by-side, stroking and kissing. "I never swallowed Nick's cum," Linda said, apropos of nothing.

"I don't care," I lied.

"He was just taunting you," she said. "Only had his pathetic needle-dick in my mouth once trying to get him hard."

"I watched you two kissing. Looked pretty hot and heavy."

"Nick was big on public displays of affection. Made him feel like some kind of pool hall Casanova."

"Not the great Latin lover?"

Linda laughed. "He was a junky," she said. "Much more interested in his next fix than fucking. Nick couldn't get it up, if you want to know the truth."

I really didn't give a shit about the truth but felt compelled to dig myself in deeper. "Thought he was your dream fantasy."

"You're my dream fantasy." Linda lifted my hand gently to her breast, holding it there with both of hers. "What I wanted all along was for you to be my knight in shining armor. To believe you'd risk anything, go through heaven and hell, to save me. And you did. Here you are after everything, here at my side. I love you, Tod. Nick was just a stupid fling. You're my soul mate."

Linda gently kissed the tip of my nose and settled against me, curled in my arms, more kitten than lioness. "What's this?" she asked, her fingertips tracing the edges of my bandage.

"Ran into a sharp pointed object."

"Poor baby," she murmured.

"You should see the other guy."

I was eager to tell her all about my street duel. Getting no reply, I saw she was fast asleep. Linda's head rested on my chest, and I felt the even rise and fall of her breathing through the soft press of her breasts against my side. The soothing rhythm augmented my own heartbeat, lulling me into slumber. I drifted off into a blissful dreamless state. Our private nightmare had come to an end.

We slept clinging together like innocent children until past sundown. I awoke first and tiptoed to the window, pulling back the curtains on a riot of color blazing across the western sky. Not a soul in sight. I stood there naked, bathed in the lurid light, enjoying the pyrotechnics. Turning back into the room, I saw Linda propped on her elbow, staring at me.

"Always were a sucker for sunsets," she said.

"I'm a sucker for you."

"I'm starving."

"How about I get them to send something up?"

"See why I love you so much. You're absolutely the best. We'll have a little hotel picnic just like the old days."

I pulled on my pants and shirt, digging my huaraches out of the duffel. "What're you hungry for?"

"Anything. Just get lots."

"Deal." I headed for the door.

"Tod . . . ?" Linda called. "You said you brought strawberries?"

"Beautiful, ripe, and delicious. Like you."

"Better get some whipped cream, too," she said. "Tons of it."

I wandered out onto the grounds unsure which way to go. Instead of asking for directions at the front desk, I found my own path by instinct. La Caldera turned out to be a big place. I roamed under the trees checking things out. Off to one side, I noticed campers parked in a row. A couple days ago, I would have spent the night there beside them in Bitter Lemon.

Between two steaming mineral water pools, a brightly lit glass-paneled building gleamed in the night. Large concrete serpents jutted from the facade like idols decorating an Aztec temple. A small hot pool fronted the place. I spotted seated diners through the tall glass walls and went inside. A bar ran along the back, bottles shining on mirrored shelves. The restaurant occupied the remainder of the room. No one noticed me. Only half the tables were occupied, all by Mexican families. After a second glance, I saw a gringo couple sitting by the tall windows overlooking the pool.

The manager approached. I assumed that's what he was. My father's place didn't have a maître d'. Not that kind of joint. The man asked where I'd like to sit. I told him I was on my honeymoon and hoped he might arrange to have our meals delivered to the room.

"*¡No problema, señor!*" he exclaimed with the simple smile he reserved for newlyweds and newborns. He showed me a handwritten menu, pointing out a special dish. "*Lechón pibil con cebollas encurtidas.*" He explained the suckling pig had been marinated in anchiote paste and the juice of Seville oranges for twenty-four hours, then wrapped in banana leaves and baked in a pit filled with fire-heated rocks. The spa raised its own pigs along with the grain to feed them. The *lechón* was the authentic traditional dish because one of the staff cooks came from Yucatán.

"*Fabulosa,*" I said, asking him to send a couple plates up to room 27.

"*¿Quiere un postre?*"

I declined his offer of dessert, asking instead for a big bowl of whipped cream to be included in the order.

"*Ah, sí,*" the man grinned. He told me whipped cream sweetened any honeymoon.

"Thought you got lost," Linda said as I let myself back into our room. She lay nude on the rumpled bed.

"I did, a little." I crossed over and sat beside her, running my hand along her thigh.

"Too many clothes," she said, plucking at the buttons on my shirt. "I need flesh."

I pushed her hand away, "Food's coming."

"Poor Toddy. Afraid the waiter will see your little ding-dong?"

A loud knock prompted Linda to scramble from the bed and sprint for the bathroom. I opened the door and a teenage kid carried in a tray with our dinners. He set them on a round table in the center of the room, plates covered with inverted soup bowls. A bud vase with a sprig of oleander added a touch of class.

I took a twenty-peso note from my wallet and way over-tipped the kid. It made his day. I figured I was living large if only for a single night.

"Coast is clear!" I called soon as he left.

Linda returned to bed, settling among the pillows. "What's on the menu?" she asked.

"Suckling pig. Want a beer?"

"¿Como no?"

"I've also got a little Herradura," I said, uncapping two Pacificos.

"Beer's fine." She smiled up at me. I set the tray down beside her. "Only naked people can partake of this feast," she said.

I unbuttoned my shirt and peeled off my pants. "Good rule," I said, sitting bare-ass across from our meal.

"You're very cute, Todolla. I like how you do everything I tell you."

We clinked beer bottles. After a first sip, I pulled my jeans off the floor and fished the pill bottle from a front pocket. "Time for my penicillin," I said, swallowing one with my next swig.

"*¿Por qué?*"

"Infection."

"VD?" she grinned.

"Knife fight." I pointed to my gauze dressing, again wanting to tell my tale of heroic combat. Linda didn't seem interested. She lifted the bowls off our plates. Sweet spicy aromas seduced us. We ate with rolled tortillas, sitting cross-legged on the bed. Best thing I'd ever tasted in my life. After mopping up the last bits, I carried the tray back to the table and took the strawberries out of the cooler.

"*So* scrumptious," Linda sighed. She uncovered the whipped cream and dipped in a sampling forefinger as I approached with the fruit.

"Taste good?" I set the basket between us.

"*Deliciosa.*"

"*Mucho mejor con las fresas.*" I dragged a strawberry through a spume of whipped cream and sucked it into my mouth. It tasted like the essence of all the fruit I'd ever eaten.

"*¡Exactamente!*" Linda mirrored my contented expression, slurping down a juicy dripping strawberry.

We laughed, feeding each other berries frothy with whipped cream. "*Con mucho gusto,*" we repeated after every mouthful, laughing harder and harder, daubing blobs of the sweet stuff on our faces. One experimental lick led to sticky kissing. I smoothed whipped cream across Linda's breasts.

She fell laughing back against the pillows and scooped a handful of foamy whiteness out of the bowl, spreading it between her legs. "You didn't get my cherry," Linda giggled, sticking a plump rosy fruit into her own pink center, "but you're welcome to my berry."

Kneeling like a supplicant, I crooned a private prayer before the sweet, spumy sanctuary. Linda's laughter gave way to low moaning when I licked with puppy-dog abandon. I siphoned the hidden strawberry into my rolled tongue. She wrapped her legs around my waist as I entered her. Kissing her hard on the lips, I pushed the pungent fruit into her mouth. Linda made a humming sound deep in her throat. She was a killer. It thrilled me. Like making love to Bonnie Parker.

We showered together, something we'd always enjoyed. Long ago at the Hotel Earle, I discovered that Linda used conditioner on her pubic hair. One of her love secrets. Wiping off the steamy mirror, I admired my manly ten o'clock shadow before shaving. After drying myself, I climbed back into my clothes. Linda took more time, sorting through dresses hanging in the antique *guardarropa*. She selected a flimsy flame-colored silk number bought years ago in Paris, pulling it on over her nakedness. "Love to go skinny-dipping." A quick smile. "Better not break any more laws."

Seeing Linda's taut nipples outlined against her gossamer dress when she leaned to pluck a bikini from the bottom dresser drawer made me grin. I dug my swimming trunks out of the duffel and guided my wife back to the restaurant.

"Fancy a drink?" Linda asked as we entered the bar.

The manager leered when he saw us climb onto a pair of tall stools. He asked if we enjoyed our dinners. The smarmy insinuation in his voice cut through his formal Spanish. I said it had been *inolvidable* and turned my back on him.

Linda and I ordered margaritas from the white-jacketed bartender. The cocktails arrived frosted and salt-rimmed. "Skoal," I said as we clinked.

"*Salud.*"

We complimented the barman. He lingered to chat, glancing shyly at Linda's silk-swathed breasts. I asked about the hot springs. He told us how to get to the dressing rooms and where to find clean towels. Each cubicle had a key on a lanyard hanging inside the door for guests to secure their valuables while they bathed.

We finished our drinks. After thanking the bartender, I paid and left a tip. "What a swell guy," I said on our way to the pool.

Linda smiled. "And such excellent taste in tits."

Another couple already splashed in the steaming water. I grabbed several skimpy towels from a stack on a poolside table as we found our way to dressing room 3. The place was cramped as a phone booth, inviting laughter and a clumsy embrace. Linda tugged her flimsy dress up over her head and pulled on her bikini. I struggled with my pants.

"See you in the pool," she whispered, kissing my cheek, out the door like an escape artist.

I soon followed. Linda clung to the metal ladder, half-submerged. "Geronimo!" I cannonballed over her head into the pool. My wife grinned, diamond-points of spray glistening in her rose-gold hair when I came up sputtering.

We paddled to the opposite side of the circular pool, far from the other couple. Hanging from our elbows, backs against the edge, we kept our voices low so they couldn't hear. The hot mineral water felt soothing as a bathtub. The bartender had told us it was good for sciatica, rheumatism, high blood pressure, and kidney ailments. He hadn't mentioned knife wounds.

"*La dolce vita,*" I said.

"Better get used to it." Linda's eyes sparkled with mischief.

"You kidding? This place probably costs over a hundred pesos a night."

"A hundred and fifty. I took twelve hundred bucks from Nick, plus our money from the bank." Linda's grin flashed with naughty pleasure. "You got something from Shank. If not, you're an idiot."

"Over three thou," I said. "Plus the watches and the Beretta."

"How many watches?"

"Four. Different makes. All pretty classy."

Linda beamed. "You see? Nearly five big ones in cash. We can score at least a grand apiece for the watches. If we sell them in the States. Keep one for yourself, of course."

"Got one with your name on it. White-gold lady's Rolex all covered in diamonds."

"Garish."

"No. Very classy. Just like you."

Linda kissed me. "You're sweet," she said, "even if you are a big fat liar."

"Give me a fucking break."

"I'm a WASP country-club bitch just like my mother." She reached underwater and slipped her hand into my trunks. "My little beatnik boy introduced me to the sordid pleasures of bohemian life." She kissed me again. "And I never wrote to thank him."

I felt myself growing hard in her knowing grip. "Wear the Rolex," I said. "Be a big hit at the country club."

"Yeah. Show those other cunts some real class." Linda gave me a gentle squeeze. "Figure three thousand dollars' worth of watches. When we sell the Pontiac to Freddy, that makes it nearly ten grand as a nest egg."

"Whoa! Slow down. What're you talking about? We can't take that car to Freddy. Not with a dead man's prints all over it."

Linda looked at me in pity. "Freddy won't know he's dead," she said. "We can wipe the car down if it makes you feel better. It was stolen in the first place. They won't find Nick for days. Maybe not for a week or more. Not a clue whose body it is. I took all his ID. Shank taught me that with Frankie. Nick looks sort of Mexican. They'll probably figure he's just another dead cholo bumped-off by his bad-ass *pachuco* amigos."

"Maybe." I still didn't buy it. "Won't Freddy be a little suspicious if it's you trying to unload the Firebird instead of Nick?"

"Why? I was with Nick when they talked about price. He said we'd be back in a week. What difference will it make if I'm the one who shows up to finish the deal? All Freddy wants is the car. He'll think Nick sent his old lady as a bag man."

"Okay," I said. It sounded risky. Nothing like what we'd just been through. Maybe a chance worth taking. "Ten Gs can buy a whole lot of freedom."

Linda wrapped her arms around my neck. "Oh, Tod, think how wonderful it would be if we had ten times more."

"If pigs could fly, there'd be no more bird-watchers."

"I'm serious. What about twenty times? A quarter million! My God, Toddy, just imagine it."

"I can imagine being president. Doesn't mean I'd get any votes."

My wife pulled back, her hands on my shoulders, regarding me with such intensity I knew further foolishness would not be tolerated. "Nick and Shank were planning a job," she said. "A big one. That's why they wanted the guns. It happened all at once when we got up to Guad. Almost by accident. If I hadn't killed Frankie, we might have missed the whole deal. I was part of their plan. They said it would be a pushover."

"So . . . ?"

"We could do it, Tod. We've got the guns. I know the plan. It's like a gift. The whole thing's been handed to us on a silver platter."

"You're nuts."

"Just listen, please." Linda bobbed on the surface a couple feet away. "There's a Swiss guy, married to a *mexicana*. They own a strawberry farm on this side of Irapuato, Fresas Suizas. The place is a front. The real business is smack. Nick and Shank knew all about it. They were always talking about the strawberry farm. Even in Barra. Even with us listening. We didn't understand one damn thing they were saying."

I tried hard to figure things out. "What is it they do?" I asked. "Grow poppies among the strawberry plants?"

"No, no," she said. "They don't grow it. The farm is like a distribution center. They cook the heroin someplace else and bring it to Fresas Suizas in bags or something. The buyers come from Europe mostly. Suitcases full of cash. Bundles of hundreds. So much money they don't even count it. They weigh it."

I laughed, energized by vibrating nerves. "What are you saying? That we should go steal a suitcase stuffed with money?" I heard the fear oscillating in my voice.

"Will you please listen to me?" Linda sounded so calm it scared me more. "They had it all worked out. Nick and Shank planned everything. Somebody tipped them off. They knew a shipment had arrived. A European buyer is in town. Driving a baby blue Ford Galaxie convertible with Jalisco plates. The buy is set for noon sharp tomorrow at the farm."

"Tip come from Freddy?"

"Don't think so. He doesn't deal in junk."

"Who was it then?"

"How should I know? I never met him. He doesn't know anything about me."

"Maybe. Maybe not. He must be in on it. He has to expect a cut."

"So what? Let him go find Nick to collect his cut."

I bounced on tiptoes, folding my arms across my chest to keep Linda from seeing me tremble. Up to my neck in hot water and it felt like I was caked in ice. "You're not really serious about this?" I said.

"Haven't you been listening?" She sounded stern. "I was in

on it all along. Part of the plan. That's why Nick bought me a gun. One you could hide easily. He called it a sneak piece. The idea was for me to go in first and case the place. The Swiss guy's wife works up front, selling strawberries. Keeps it looking legit. If she's all alone, my job was to chat her up and get her away from any hidden alarm. Then, pull the gun and keep her quiet."

"What if other people are inside buying strawberries?" I couldn't believe I was hearing all this.

"I'd go outside right away and pretend to take pictures. Nick and Shank'd see me with the camera and know not to make their play. When the last customer left, I'd go back in and take the wife hostage. The banditos do their gangster thing. We march *mamacita* out where the deal is going down. The Swiss guy rolls over without a fight. He'd never risk seeing his wife get hurt."

"How can you be so damn sure it's on for noon sharp tomorrow? This is Mexico, for Christ's sake."

"We're dealing with the Swiss here. They run their trains on time. None of this *mañana* bullshit for them."

I didn't know what to say, thinking she was putting me on until I remembered everything that went down in the crypt under the *panteón* that morning. Linda's cold efficiency. An unidentified creepy feeling came over me. I wondered if she'd planned it all in advance. Something was wrong with her plan, but I couldn't figure out just what. Worse, I didn't want to try.

"Don't you think it'll be a little obvious," I asked. "Pulling a stickup in a bright red getaway car? Even the Federales aren't dumb enough to miss the gangster-mobile."

"That's the beauty part." Linda smiled like she'd just aced

her finals. "Nobody's going to call the cops and complain about drug money getting ripped off. Nick and Shank planned on grabbing all the heroin, too. I think they wanted the horse more than the dough. I don't know if we should take the dope. Probably more trouble to unload than it's worth."

"Wouldn't it make better sense to wait until the buyers leave with the smack? They're bound to be the muscle. Why not go in and grab the cash after they split?"

"Nick and Shank said it wouldn't be smart to wait. Said not to give anybody time to lock the dough up in a safe."

"You talk like this is a done deal."

"Tod, think about it. We could buy a house on Telegraph Hill. Or one in the Village. Some brick Federal beauty on a tree-lined street. The perfect place to finish your novel. Isn't that what you always wanted?"

It was exactly what I'd always wanted. I'd dreamed of it since I was a little kid. My father made bets and bankrolled card games all his life. He never got a shot at a score this big. "Would be real nice," I said. "A sweet place on Bedford Street."

"What would it cost? Fifty grand? Sixty?" Linda's face radiated pure joy. "There'd still be more than a hundred left over. We'd be set for life, Toddy."

I wasn't so sure. The original plan had two torpedoes for backup. Now, there was only me. I tried explaining this to Linda. "I'm not Shank. Not even close."

"Doesn't matter," she said. "The key to the whole thing is the wife. With her as a hostage, Donald Duck could pull it off."

"Maybe so," I said, not really convinced. "Nice to know you still believe in me."

Linda folded her arms around my neck. "Why don't we sleep on it? Things aren't so scary in the daylight." She kissed me, a long lingering embrace. "I want you to fuck me again," she whispered in my ear.

We toweled dry and hurried through the darkness to our room. In bed after I changed my wet bandage, our urgency subsided as we held each other, bodies joining gently together. No dominance or submission, only familiar warmth and happiness. Linda fell asleep almost the moment our lovemaking ended. I watched her peaceful steady breathing, amazed at her tranquillity. Thinking about what she proposed sent shudders of apprehension vibrating through me. How could she sleep innocently while I trembled with fear? I knew I didn't have to go through with it. I could walk away from the whole thing in the morning. But that would mean walking out on Linda. Kissing our marriage good-bye.

My mind raced with conflicting thoughts. Perhaps the whole thing was some elaborate hoax? Linda said she wanted a knight in shining armor. Someone who'd risk everything for her. A stern test of love. Was she once again asking me to prove myself worthy? Maybe there was no crime planned. All Linda wanted was loyalty. Right from the start she'd seemed an unobtainable goddess. A fairy-tale princess from the unfamiliar world of wealth and privilege. I'd won her love by being a rogue, not a prince. She'd just upped the ante. No longer enough to play the vagabond troubadour. I had to ride the outlaw trail. It was all in. Time to bet the limit.

EASTER
THURSDAY

—⁓ • ● • ⁓—

I awoke to sunlight flooding through the parted drapes. Linda bustled about the room packing stuff into several woolen *bolsas*. She wore a short-sleeved white cotton peasant blouse bright with Huichol embroidery and a denim miniskirt showing off her shapely tanned legs. I loved watching her move, the flex of her slender arms, a slight swell in her calves as she bent to pick something off the floor, the gentle push of her bare breasts beneath the blouse. She felt my eyes upon her.

"Enjoying yourself, sleepyhead?" An approving grin.

"*Sí, señorita.*"

"I'm no *señorita*. I'm a respectable married woman."

"Respectable? Don't push it."

Linda lost interest in mindless banter. She gave me a long appraising stare. "Well . . . ?" she asked.

"Well, what?" I knew what she meant.

"Are you in or out?"

"Count me in." I answered without hesitation. "Maybe just a couple questions."

"Ask away. There's coffee beside the bed. *Pan de huevo, también.*"

I rolled over and saw the tray. Coffeepot and an empty cup, a pitcher of hot milk, sugar-coated pastries. "How long have you been up?" I filled the cup and placed a penicillin pill in my mouth.

"Long enough to walk to the restaurant and back."

"Okay." I leaned against the wooden headboard with my coffee. "I get the plan. Take the wife hostage. Hubby rolls over without a fight. What about whoever's buying the smack? Maybe more than one. They'll have guns and won't give a shit about Mrs. Swiss Guy."

"All figured out," Linda said, calm and confident. "Shank said the trick is to go in loud. Take them by surprise. Before they know what's happening. You're shouting, 'Hands up! Down on the floor! Get the fuck down or you're dead!' Yell it in Spanish, too. Loud and fast. Shank swore they'd do what you told them. It's psychological."

Psychology, my ass. It sounded like a cheap gangster flick.

I didn't tell Linda that. "So, they're lying on the floor. Then what? Suppose they talk things over and decide they can take us?"

"That won't happen. Simon says hands behind backs." Linda reached into her leather shoulder bag. "Then tie them up." She pulled out a roll of duct tape. "With this. It's quick. Couple turns around their wrists. Unbreakable. Slap a strip across their mouths. They can't make a sound. In case unexpected strawberry customers come nosing around."

Linda had the self-assurance of a master mechanic instructing her apprentice in the use of a torque wrench. Never having done anything like it before didn't seem to faze her. She sounded so confident she almost had me convinced. "Just might work," I said.

"'Course it will," she cheerfully replied. "We're going to be rich."

Linda spoke with such determination I had to believe her. The warmth in her voice drenched me with love. I feared losing her much more than death.

"Rich is nice," I said. "What's important is we loved each other when we were poor."

Linda gave me her spare-us-this-sentimental-cornball-shit look. "I've been thinking about the dope," she said in a matter-of-fact manner. "Maybe it's a mistake to leave it behind. Wouldn't look right to the cops. Better to take it like professionals. We could always dump the shit or turn it into cash somehow. Met some sleazebags in Guad. Friends of Nick. They might want bargain-basement horse."

"I don't know," I said. "Showing up with that much for sale is like advertising we just ripped off the strawberry farm."

"You're right," she said. "Better to ditch it."

"Want to hole-up in some cheap pad and get hooked?"

"Like I didn't get enough of that watching Nick." Linda sat beside me on the bed, tracing her fingers along my bare knee. "No good reason for you to trust me. Never mind I love you and you love me. Words come easy. Only actions count. I ran off with Nick. Left you drunk in bed beside a bitch I killed. Why should you ever trust me again?"

"Yesterday's news," I said.

"Very noble even if it's bullshit." Linda squeezed my knee. "Here's the deal. After the job, we each take off in our own car. Meet up back at the Fenix. Get separate rooms so Freddy won't know we're together. We play it fair and square at the farm. Go in carrying our own *bolsas*. Split the cash up inside, on the spot. That way, if you decide to cut out, or maybe if I do, we both get an equal share."

"Linda, honey, it's okay. I'm on your side."

"You shouldn't be. Not a hundred percent. Not after all that's gone down. Let's do it my way. We split the cash up front. If I see you at the Fenix, I'll know you really love me."

"You're so full of crap. I'll be there. You know that." I stared at her unable to fathom her emotions, knowing all the while it was impossible.

Linda kissed me. "Change your mind, you'll still have half the take."

"Without you, it's not worth a damn."

"Don't bet on it."

I swung out of bed and crossed naked to the dresser where Shank's satchel rested. Fishing inside, I pulled out the lady's Rolex, diamonds glittering, and slipped it over Linda's slim wrist. "So you'll know what time to meet me at the Fenix," I said.

"It's beautiful," she said. "Can't wait to rub it in the noses of those country-club sluts." Linda's eyes danced. "All right. Your turn. Let's see the choices."

I laid the remaining three watches out on the dresser top. "An embarrassment of riches," I said.

"I like this one." Linda picked the lizard-banded Patek Phillipe.

"Too delicate." I took off my cheap Timex and tugged on the Rolex Oyster Perpetual. "This one I can wear surfing. We'll have not-quite matching Rolexes."

"Let's synchronize them." She laughed. "Like they do in the movies."

I changed my bandage and dressed quickly. It didn't take long to pack. Our worldly possession didn't amount to all that much. After hauling down the cooler and my duffel and locking them in the van, I helped Linda carry her bulging woven sacks to the Firebird.

"The tab's on me," she said. "My treat."

"If the lady insists."

"Meet you in front of the strawberry farm in an hour. Twelve o'clock sharp. Swiss Fanatic Time. Fresas Suizas, remember?"

"How could I forget?"

"I need one small favor."

"My pleasure."

Linda hauled a cheap vinyl suitcase out of the trunk. "Still have that war-surplus shovel?" I nodded. "Great. This is Nick's stuff. Get rid of it. Please. Bury it someplace along the road."

"I can handle it."

"We don't want stray dogs digging shit up." I promised to plant the suitcase deeper than King Tut's tomb. "Put a curse on him while you're at it." Linda's quick grin gave way to a frown. "I've reconsidered how to get our money back into the States. I wanted to travel in style. Sell both cars. Fly back first-class. Total *decadencia*. Problem is, there's this law, I think, where you have to declare any cash you're bringing in. Over a certain amount. Wouldn't be cool if customs found a couple hundred grand in our luggage."

"Bummer."

"Best plan is driving home in Bitter Lemon. We'll cut holes in the bottom of the foam rubber to hide the cash. The van has to be completely clean. No dope. No seeds, no stems. Nothing a dog might sniff out. You'll have to get a haircut. Young couple coming home from a cheap vacation."

"Too bad about all that Michoacán." I meant it as a joke.

"Christ! You're such an idiot." Linda had no patience for foolishness. "Sell it! Throw it away with the heroin. Maybe smoke yourself silly for the next few days. Just do me one favor. Don't get high until after we pull off this job."

"Scout's honor," I said.

"Good." Linda grabbed me for a long passionate kiss.

"Time to earn your merit badge. I'll fuck your brains out at the Fenix."

I drove slowly back toward Irapuato on Highway 110 checking the sides of the road for a safe place to bury Nick's suitcase. Good to have this simple task. Took my mind off what lay ahead. An unknown future provided little consolation.

After five or six miles, I came to a wooded stream, a dark green zigzag between purple alfalfa fields. I pulled off the road, got out, and scoped the scene under the guise of taking a piss. No one around. Not a house in sight. I took the suitcase and the trenching shovel and locked the van. Before another car appeared on the highway, I wove my way through the creek-side thicket.

A hundred yards in, I came to a place where the stream bank cut bare and steep. I dug high above the feeble trickle, fearing a rainy season flash flood might wash my work away. The forest floor soil felt soft and thick. My shovel carved easily through. I pretended I was digging Nick's grave. Better to bury the corpse instead of his suitcase. I didn't share Linda's optimism. His body might be found anytime. Easy to imagine Nick already stretched out on a slab in the Guanajuato police morgue.

In twenty minutes, I dug a hole, more of a trench really, at the top edge of the cutbank. I shoved in the vinyl suitcase, simple as stashing it in a bus station coin locker. Filling the hole back up with dirt was easy. I wedged rocks into the bank-side opening and scattered leaves over the top surface. Things looked undisturbed. No one would ever find it.

A two-ton farm truck approached as I reached the road. I stayed hidden in the bushes until it passed. After storing the shovel, I was back in gear chugging toward Irapuato. There seemed only three possible outcomes: death, jail, or life on easy street. I focused on the third, imagining the beautiful brick town house I'd dreamed about when I was a kid.

Something troubled me. I tried putting my finger on just what was wrong. Then I saw the painted sign FRESAS SUIZAS. A snowcapped row of jagged cartoon mountains outlined the top. Dead center, a big red comic book strawberry with a smiling face winked at me under a feathered Tyrolean hat. I'd missed it both times driving past before. Seemed like a dumb place to die.

Turning off by the silly grinning fruit, I followed a single-lane dirt road straight as a carpenter's chalk line through the berry fields. It was a couple minutes past noon. After nearly a mile, I came to a packed-earth parking area set far back from the pink strawberry store. The red Firebird sat next to a baby-blue Ford Galaxie convertible sporting Jalisco license plates. I pulled into the space alongside. The deal was going down. All around, the broad green crop sweltered in the late-morning heat. Linda leaned against the Pontiac's front fender smoking a cigarette. I'd never seen her smoke tobacco. She'd always claimed to be allergic to it.

I climbed out of the VW, making a crack about habit-forming substances. She flicked the butt away into the surrounding berries. A spiral of sparks like a miniature comet. "Learned a lot of bad habits from Nick," she said, her hawk's stare unblinking. "You're late."

"Busy burying your boyfriend's suitcase."

Linda didn't flinch. "Never my boyfriend." Her eyes daggered into mine. "More like a mentor."

I wanted to say what else did he teach you? How to swallow? Choking it back, I muttered, "Always helps when someone shows you the ropes."

"We're in luck." She pointed at the Ford. "Engine's still hot. Must have just got here." She opened her *bolsa*, displaying the little Browning and a roll of duct tape. "Got your heater?"

Talking like a double-feature dropper's dame didn't make her the real thing. And then, it dawned on me. What troubled my mind all along. "Look," I said. "I know these guys can't go to the law after we take them off. But they'll know all about us. What we look like. What we drive. Bitter Lemon and a flashy red Firebird won't be hard to spot. They'll put the word out. Every cheap killer in Mexico will come looking for a piece of us. Don't you see? We can't go to Freddy or any other crook in Guad. We'll be on the world's worst wanted list."

"Cool it a minute, will you?" Linda spoke with calm determination. "Shank worked everything out. No witnesses. Nobody alive to finger us."

"You're crazy," I said.

"No. It's easy. They'll be lying face down. Hands tied. Shoot them one at a time in the back of the head. Like swatting flies."

"Flies don't beg for mercy."

"They'll have gags over their mouths."

"Cold-blooded."

"Shit, Tod, if you can't do it, I will. Where's your gun?"

Moving like a mechanical automaton, I pulled the Beretta out of Shank's satchel. "Good," Linda said. "If there's any problem, I'll step back outside. If you don't see me, wait five min-utes before coming in." She walked toward the one-story pink stucco building, her leather bag slung over one shoulder. Half-way, she paused, turning back to look at me. "You can do it," Linda called. "I love you."

I watched her walk the rest of the way, open the screen door below a sign reading FRESAS and slip through into darkness.

Even then, I knew I didn't have to do it. I could climb into Bitter Lemon and just drive off. Keep on living my aimless nothing life. Wasn't like anyone was forcing me. I shoved the automatic into my waistband and dug my lucky Olympic coin out of a front pocket, staring at the image of the plumed Aztec ballplayer. The losing team in those games was sacrificed. Sometimes they used a severed human head for a ball.

Sick at heart, I scaled the silver disc high into the air. It glittered with sunlight, arcing over the strawberry field, bright as a little falling star. I watched it disappear into the rows of green. Should have cleared the hell out. Instead, I stood in the hot midday Mexican sun, staring at the strawberry-colored building shimmering like pale fire in the blaze of noon. I didn't see another soul for what felt like forever, an empty straw *bolsa* clamped under my left arm. Five hot minutes went by. I checked my fancy Rolex, pulled back the slide on the Beretta, and headed into the unknown.

It was the longest walk of my life. I trudged those fifty yards like the last mile to the hot seat, trying to work things out in my mind every slow step of the way. Linda was wrong. No need to kill anybody. None of them knew what kind of cars we drove. Might take hours before they worked themselves free. We'd be long gone. No selling the Firebird to Freddy but what difference did that make? Always another crooked big shot with a taste for flashy cars on the road home.

Wished I'd thought all this through last night when Linda spelled out Shank's great plan. Should've worn bandannas for the heist like old-time Western outlaws. Linda could have gone in with hers covering her hair and pulled it down over her face when she took the wife hostage. Good old hindsight. Always 20/20 on the eye chart.

Everything remained dark behind the screen door when I swung it open, not knowing what to expect inside. I stood in the cool shadows of the entrance as my eyes adjusted, the air sweetened with a pungent aroma of fruit. Produce stands stacked with boxes of strawberries were the first thing I saw. Next, I spotted Linda. She stood behind a short Mexican woman whose fear-widened eyes gleamed above the silver strip of duct tape plastered over her mouth. My wife pressed the muzzle of her tiny pistol to the terrified woman's right temple.

"Thought you'd changed your mind," Linda said. "Here. Take this." Using her left hand, Linda pulled the fat roll of tape from inside her shoulder bag. "Tie her up."

"Okay."

"*Date la vuelta*," Linda ordered the cowering wife, and she turned meekly around, placing her hands behind her back.

I bound them together with three wraps of tape. The air felt radioactive.

"I've been thinking things over," I said.

"No time for that now."

"Listen. Thing is, we don't have to follow through with that last part of the plan. What we talked about outside." I didn't want to mention killing anybody in case the Mexican woman understood English. "They haven't seen our cars so they won't know what we drive. Get them on the floor fast enough and no one takes a really good look at us. Just another gringo couple. We all look alike."

"Let's go," Linda said, pushing her hostage on ahead.

"Were you listening to what I said?" I put the tape into my *bolsa*.

"I heard you. Time to get it done."

Left hand on the Mexican woman's shoulder, the other holding her little Browning between the twin black braids, Linda whispered instructions to her frightened hostage. I heard her say, "*la oficina*" and "*donde guarda las drogas*." Wasn't sure if she got the lingo just right. What did I know? Linda's Spanish was way better than mine.

The *mexicana* was savvy to the message and led us out back of the strawberry store into a corrugated metal warehouse arching over bare ground. A tractor, a couple plows, a disc cultivator, and a bunch of other large unfamiliar farming hulks filled the space. Double rolling garage doors at the far end were pulled down tight. Against the opposite wall, hemmed in by stacks of empty wooden strawberry boxes, a windowless plywood shed stood raw and fresh as a new packing crate. It looked like someplace where a farmer might store pesticide.

Seemed an unlikely spot for a big drug deal but that's where the *patrona* led us, weaving between rusting machinery retired for spare parts, a graveyard of forgotten farm implements. An open padlock hung by its shackle from the hasp staple on the closed shed door. A cement block provided a step up. When we reached the entrance, Linda turned to me. "Open it," she whispered. "Then step aside and follow me in."

My heart raced. She was in charge and I obeyed her orders. I still trusted the bond of our love. Believed in the end she'd listen to reason. I stepped up, took hold of the knob with my left hand, and yanked the door open. An industrial phosphorescent light fixture hung flush against the low ceiling. Linda shoved our gagged and bound prisoner inside. "*¡Abajo!*" she shouted. "*¡Todos apoyados en el suelo!*"

I ran in behind them, waving the Beretta in the air and yelling, "Get down! Flat on the floor! Pronto!"

Like a magic trick, all three behaved exactly as Shank said they would, dropping to their knees on command. The Swiss guy was dressed like a hick in tan Carhartt bib overalls and a faded denim shirt. He stared up at his captive wife, face taut with fear. The other two wore dark business suits. When Linda barked, "*¡Sobre sus estómagos!*" they all obeyed, silently stretching out flat on their bellies. "*¡Manos detrás de sus espaldas!*" she ordered and they all bent their arms behind their backs. "Guard the door," Linda shouted to an imaginary unseen accomplice. "Don't let anyone in."

I marveled at her impromptu ingenuity. She caught my eye and jerked her head. A slight gesture demanding I get on with it. The moment I dreaded. I thrust the automatic into my waistband above the sheathed Randall thinking it would be safer there in case one of them tried something heroic. Pulling the roll of duct tape from my *bolsa*, I started with the pale Swiss, remembering a Mexican dish called *enchiladas suizas*. Made with chicken, white cheese, and a cream sauce. A bland affair compared to the rest of Mexico's fiery cuisine.

I wrapped a couple turns of tape around the farmer's wrists. He stared helplessly at his wife through steel-rimmed bifocals. "*Ich flehe Sie An tun Sie meiner Frau nichts an!*" he pleaded. "Not hurt the wife. I beg of you." With his wispy light-brown hair and frog-belly complexion, he seemed the living embodiment of those insipid *enchiladas*.

I moved swiftly to the next guy, a burly bald Mediterranean fellow sporting a thick black mustache. He growled at me in Italian, sputtering with rage as I wrapped tape around his wrists. I didn't understand what he said but caught the word *morto* and knew he wasn't wishing me a long life.

The third man was tall and rangy with close-cropped hair so blond it looked to be spun from sunlight. His angular features reminded me of the doomed Swedish knight in *The Seventh Seal*. "This is a bad mistake," he said in a voice almost without accent. "You have not given the matter proper thought." I bound his hands together extra tight. "Why risk almost certain—" I slapped a strip of tape over his mouth, silencing the soft-spoken threats.

In a matter of seconds, I had gags plastered over the lips of the other two as well.

The Italian wouldn't have much fun when he got around to yanking the tape off his organ grinder's mustache.

Linda told the *mexicana* to kneel and lie on the floor next to her husband. She did it without hesitation. I felt a surge of exhilaration vibrate through me. Everything was going off without a hitch, exactly as planned. Maybe we'd get away with it after all. "Better check and see if they're armed," Linda said, easily as if asking me to pass the salt.

Why didn't I think of that? Once again, my risk-taking wife was ahead of the game and called the shots. "Okay," I said, kneeling to pat down our captives. I took a folding clasp-knife and a pair of vise grips from the side pockets of the farmer's overalls and dropped them in my *bolsa*. The Italian growled and grunted as I frisked him. Sounded like a mad dog trying to chew his way through the gag. At the crease of his back, I found a waistband holster. "Bingo!" I smiled up at Linda, showing her a snub-nose .38 revolver like the one Shank used to kill Doc. Easy imagining Guido getting at it when we weren't looking. His hands were taped right over where he carried his piece. "What should I do with this?"

"Keep it," she said. "I like this one." She flashed the baby Browning's mother-of-pearl grips. "More ladylike."

The Swedish movie star came up clean. The Italian's snub nose went into my sack with the other stuff. I took a look around the shed's plywood interior. No decorations aside from a tequila Cuervo calendar tacked to one wall. The big show spread across a large worktable. It was something to behold.

Fat bricks of plastic-wrapped snow-white heroin stood randomly stacked on either side of a triple-beam balance scale. One of them rested on the pan. I figured they each weighed a kilo. A rough count came to about fifty. That made more than a hundred pounds of pure horse.

I had no idea of the value. After cutting it many times, probably millions. Five years ago, a big drug bust in New York came up with a hundred pounds of French smack. The cops said it would bring thirty-four million out on the street. One look in their open Samsonite briefcase told me what these two European dealers thought the shit was worth. The black hard-shell case sat on the worktable, bottom half paved with bundled US banknotes. The stacked money sat in five rows of three. Linda's eyes widened with excitement, green as the waiting cash. "Holy shit," she whispered.

I picked up a banded bundle and riffled through the currency with my thumb. All in hundreds. Without counting, I guessed there had to be at least a hundred bills in all. "Ten grand," I told my wife, waving the greenbacks like a trophy.

"Jesus Fucking Christ!" Linda seemed in shock. She reached out her left hand like someone groping in the dark. The little sneak piece glittered in her right. Very slowly, Linda pulled three more bundles from the corner of the briefcase where I'd grabbed the first. I saw her eyes widen further as she did the mental math. Sixty bundles. I met her astonished gaze. Six hundred grand.

"Let's divvy up," she said, waving her little automatic like a queen with a royal scepter. "Take thirty for yourself and dump the other half in my *bolsa*." There was no way she was letting go of that baby Browning.

Heart racing, I counted out thirty bundles into my sack and checked the accordion file in the upper half of the briefcase. Nothing there. Every compartment empty as a dead man's eyes. Linda dropped thirty thousand dollars into her *bolsa*, letting each packet fall one at a time from her left hand. She enjoyed it. Like sifting gold dust through her fingers. I watched Linda's happy smile when I upended the briefcase and poured the rest of the loot into her sack.

"Time to finish the job," she said. "Where's your gun?"

"I . . . Wait a minute . . ." Without thinking, I pulled the Beretta from the back of my waistband.

"No time to wait. We've got to go."

I glanced around spotting a pair of large leather two-suiters sitting by the wall. "Lucky for us they brought suitcases. Makes hauling the horse out that much easier."

"Work to be done before we pack." Linda's predatory eyes probed deep into mine. "Two for you," she said. "Two for me."

"We don't have to do it." I was desperate, stalling for time. "Listen to me. We've got the money. We can just pack up the shit and take off. There's a padlock on the shed door. Let's lock them in. Disable their cars. You know, yank the distributors and spark plug wires. It'll take hours for them to get free. I'll wrap more duct tape around their wrists. Bind their ankles, too. Leave them locked inside with no transportation. We'll be hundreds of miles away. They won't know where to look."

Linda's implacable stare cut through my gasping pleas. Her cold expression never changed. My words made no more impression on her than raindrops bouncing off the plated hide of a crocodile. She didn't hear a thing I'd said. "I'll make it easy for you." Linda's voice betrayed no hint of emotion. The same monotone she used down among the mummies to describe cutting Frankie's throat. "I'll off the wife."

"No!"

"Do three of them all by myself. But you've got to finish it. The last one is yours. We're in this together."

"Linda, please . . ."

She pushed past me, the tiny automatic almost hidden in her delicate hand. "Out of my way, pussyboy."

"Don't! Don't do it!" Even at that moment, I still believed she wouldn't kill anyone. Only another weird test of my loyalty. "I'll do anything for you," I pleaded, "but not this."

"Big deal." She gave me a look way beyond contempt. "You just told them my name. Don't need some stupid lapdog. I want a man who'll back me up when the chips are down. If you're that guy, prove it!" Linda straightened her right arm, aiming at the back of the woman's head. "Like this!" The gagged strawberry farmer strained to stare up at her, his pleading eyes white with terror.

"No!" I lunged and knocked Linda's hand aside as she fired. The Browning made a little *pop* not much louder than a cap gun. Her aim went wide. The bullet splintered into the floorboards above the *mexicana*'s head.

"Chickenshit bastard!" Linda turned and shot me. I felt a piercing blow on my left side a split second before hearing any sound. Like getting hit by a tiny fist. "Are you fucking crazy?" I shouted.

She shot me in the stomach. It burned like the venom of a thousand hornets. A red rage enclosed me. Linda gripped her pistol with both hands, raising her aim for a headshot. She meant to kill me.

"Bitch!" I shot her square in the chest, pulling the trigger again and again and again in a blind fury. The shots rang out inside the little room like demonic thunder. In that insane instant, time stood still. The only sound an echo of gunfire ringing in my ears. Frozen in place, an insect trapped in ice, I didn't believe any of this was real. The hostages lay face down on the floor, afraid to look up, dreading who might be next to die. It all drained out of me, hatred, love, anger, fear. I looked into a bleak new world. A purgatory without hope.

Linda sprawled on her back, arms and legs ungainly splayed. She stared up at the ceiling, her embroidered Huichol blouse blotched with blood, a discarded surgical rag. I stumbled toward her and knelt by her side knowing all the while she was dead. Saw enough death this past week not to recognize it staring me in the face.

"Forgive me," I whispered, reaching out to close her emerald eyes, one eyelid after the other. I brushed my fingers across her beautiful freckled cheek. She felt warm and alive. As shocking as the ice-cold touch of Frankie's corpse. All gone now. Everything lost forever.

I staggered past our bound captives, each one alone with their thoughts, wondering why they were still alive. Stepping out of the plywood shed in a daze, I left it all behind. Money, heroin, every happiness I'd ever known. I zombie-walked like a man in a trance through the metal warehouse and out of Fresas Suizas into the blinding sacrificial glare of the Mexican sun.

Halfway to the parking area, I felt the weight of the Beretta gripped in my hand like some alien creature sucking life from my body. Hating it, I hurled the evil instrument far into the strawberry fields. Way out there somewhere with my unlucky silver coin.

The bad shit hit me all at once back in Bitter Lemon. Waves of grief welled up from deep inside. I sobbed like a lost child. In the end, every tear ever shed in the tragic history of the world would never wash away this terrible moment. Crying without control, I put the van in gear and rumbled down the dusty road toward the highway.

The physical pain started coming on just outside Irapuato. A throbbing ache in my gut amplified by waves of nausea. I drove slowly through town gritting my teeth. The little boys selling strawberries spotted me and ran alongside the VW, shouting and waving. I went straight past not giving them a glance, tears of rage blurring my vision. They kept up the chase for several blocks, a little ragamuffin mob in the rearview mirror. I never wanted to taste another goddamned strawberry again in my life.

By the time I reached the hilltop above Guanajuato, pain tore through me like wildfire. Driving made it worse. I pulled over and fished a bottle of Dilaudid out of Shank's satchel, popping four tablets in my mouth and swallowing them down with spit. Sitting absolutely still, I tried not to think, waiting for the downers to kick in. Violent agonizing tremors shot through my middle overriding all else, even never-ending grief.

I welcomed the pain. Better than mental agony. Linda dead on the farm shed floor. Our life together erased in an instant. The moment I killed her was lost to me. Not even a memory. Only blind rage exploding in my brain. Everything gone in a heartbeat. Had no anger left. Harbored only loss. Better if she'd killed me. No lingering regrets. No lifelong sadness.

Maybe fifteen minutes went by before I felt the soft warm narcotic embrace blunt my pain. The ache in my stomach faded to a muffled throb, an echo of something far away. Moving in a mist, I dug around under the sleeping platform. Clean white T-shirt. First-aid kit. Filled a Thermos with bottled water bought a million years ago in Barra. Felt like an observer watching from a distance. Unbuttoned my blood-soaked Hawaiian shirt. First shot entered far down on the left side of my chest. Thought it broke a rib and deflected. Exit wound larger than the little hole where the bullet went in. Gingerly ran my fingers around a ragged tear.

Second shot much worse. Slightly below my navel. A bit to the right. Bloody puckering puncture like another bellybutton. Bullet penetrated my intestines. Little thing. Not much bigger than a .22 shell. Leaking poisonous shit inside my body. Stupid way to die. Like stepping on a rusty nail.

I cleaned myself up with alcohol-soaked gauze pads. Taped double-thick bandages over my wounds. Gobs of Neosporin. Pulling on a clean shirt felt therapeutic. Somehow it made a difference. I needed to get to a big city hospital pronto. Guanajuato way too close to the crime scene. Best chance was a straight shot up to the border. Gulf roadmap accordioned along the car seat. Charted most direct route north. Drugs made it hard to focus. All the little red lines blurring together.

Figured the whole trip under 600 miles. If I made good time. Could be in Texas tomorrow midday. Fifteen hours of driving. Plus a little shuteye. Had all the painkillers I needed. Plenty of penicillin.

Drip. Drip. Drip. Poisonous crap leaking out of a hole in my guts. Little sips of water to wet my lips. Beer off-limits. Weed okay. Count your blessings instead of sheep. Gentlemen, start your engines. Pedal to the metal. On my way to nowhere once again.

Over the summit in second gear. Jazz tunes echoed in memory. *Don't mean a thing if it ain't got that swing.* Riffing down into the valley. *Ooo-bop-sha-bam!* Rolling farmland all around. Coyotes howl. Lizard claws scratch the sand. Seemed like forever before I cruised through Dolores Hidalgo an hour later. Birthplace of Mexican independence. September 16. Way back when. Down Mexico way. Twin red rosebuds bloomed through my clean white shirt. Blood moons. Somewhere there's music. Passed ugly new stone monument center of traffic circle. Far side of town. She sighed when she whispered *mañana.* Statue of Father Hidalgo (bronze) next in line. Nothing works out the way you plan for it. Heroic revolutionary Padre Miguel took his last breath facing a Spanish firing squad. The deck is always stacked against you.

ACKNOWLEDGMENTS

Profound thanks to my tireless agent, Ben Camardi of the Harold Matson Company; and to my talented editor, Maggie Crawford; and most especially to my loving wife, Janie Camp, for all her encouragement and support.

ABOUT THE AUTHOR

William Hjortsberg is the author of five novels, including *Falling Angel*, an Edgar Award nominee, and *Nevermore*, as well as the biography *Jubilee Hitchhiker: The Life and Times of Richard Brautigan*. Hjortsberg lives in Montana.

EBOOKS BY WILLIAM HJORTSBERG

FROM OPEN ROAD MEDIA

Available wherever ebooks are sold

CPSIA information can be obtained at www.ICGtesting.com
Printed in the USA
BVOW05s1322130515

400243BV00005B/174/P